What Happened to Ivy

What Happened to Ivy

KATHY STINSON

Second Story Press

Library and Archives Canada Cataloguing in Publication

Stinson, Kathy
What happened to Ivy / Kathy Stinson.

Issued also in an electronic format.

ISBN 978-1-926920-81-8

I. Title.

PS8587.T56W43 2012   jC813'.54   C2012-904020-7

Edited by Jonathan Schmidt
Copyedited by Lynda Guthrie
Cover and text design by Melissa Kaita
Cover photo © iStockphoto
Printed and bound in Canada

*Second Story Press gratefully acknowledges the support of the
Ontario Arts Council and the Canada Council for the Arts for our
publishing program. We acknowledge the financial support of the
Government of Canada through the Canada Book Fund.*

Published by
Second Story Press
20 Maud Street, Suite 401
Toronto, Ontario, Canada
M5V 2M5
www.secondstorypress.ca

To Robert and Tracy
whose stories haunt me still

Chapter 1

"Where are *you* going?" Mom looks at me over a laundry basket heaping with clothes.

"Hannah's."

"I need you to go to the mall and pick up Ivy's prescription."

"Can't you do it? Or Dad?"

Mom sighs. "It's just this one thing, David. It's not a big deal."

Dad steps out of his study. "Problem?"

"Why do *I* have to get Ivy's prescription?"

"Because I've got twenty essays to mark." Dad's using his best hotshot Classics professor tone of voice on me. "Your mom needs me to get Ivy's sheets on the line as soon as they come out of the washer because the dryer broke down on the last load, *and* because we're expecting an important phone call from one of Ivy's doctors."

"Yeah, yeah. It's about *Ivy*, so of course it's important."

Of course it's not important that Hannah has asked me over for the first time since she and her mom moved in three weeks ago, or that it means she might not have been hanging out with my family only because our parents know each other and there's nothing better to do.

"That's just for starters, David, but you go on ahead to Hannah's. Enjoy yourself. Just don't be long. You can go get the prescription when you get back."

"Fine."

"And you can take Ivy to the mall with you."

Not fine. Ivy at the mall is never fine. And Ivy at the mall on a Saturday when it's especially busy? But at least he hasn't stopped me going to Hannah's. And at least Ivy's busy with her physio people so he can't insist I take her with me now.

"Don't forget, David," Dad says as I push open the front door, "you *are* a member of this family."

Right. Whenever it's convenient I am.

I trudge down Ivy's wheelchair ramp, past the garden

that's become mine to take care of the last couple of years, and cross the street.

Okay, so it's not surprising that with Ivy like she is, my parents need me to help out a lot. But a bit of credit would be nice. Like 'What a great brother, playing with your sister when you could be down at the video arcade.' Or, 'We're sorry your friends haven't wanted to come over again after Ivy smushed snot onto her palm and showed it to them before she licked it off.' I mean, Ivy's not some adorable little preschooler. She's eleven years old. Thing is, my parents don't know half of what I put up with.

Hannah's dog greets me at the door first with a wide-open, golden-retriever grin. Then Hannah. Her runner's legs are long and lean. Her shiny hair just brushes her tanned shoulders. I'll never have a chance with her as anything more than a nice guy to hang with once in a while, but that's okay. Even that's a big step up for me in the grand, you know, social-hierarchy scheme of things.

"This is Shamus," Hannah says as her dog circles around my legs. He runs off and comes back with a stuffed monkey hanging out of his mouth.

I lean down and pat him. Dogs are so easy.

A pizza arrives right behind me.

"I went ahead and ordered," Hannah says.

"Fine by me. As long as there's no pineapple on it, I'm happy."

Hannah laughs. "Sorry." She opens the box and the pizza is smothered with ham and pineapple. "Hawaiian's my favorite." She laughs again, but it's almost as if she finds the fact I've said exactly the wrong thing charming instead of obnoxious.

"So," she says, "my mom was pretty surprised to find out she'd bought a house right across the street from an old friend from nursing school."

"Yeah, what are chances of that happening?"

"Is your mom still in nursing?" Hannah asks.

"No, she had to quit. Ivy takes a lot out of her."

We munch away on our pizza. I don't dislike pineapple as much as I thought.

"She's a handful, eh? Your sister?"

"Yeah. Sometimes."

On the table, on top of a stack of papers, is a brochure that looks familiar. I pick it up to see if it's for the music camp I think it is. "I was supposed to go to this camp," I tell Hannah.

"I went earlier this summer," she says, "before we moved here. It was great. How come you didn't go?"

"Insurance stopped paying for Ivy's pool therapy and

my parents decided that keeping up her therapy was more important than my music camp."

"Bummer." Hannah licks pizza sauce off her fingers. "Just think. If you'd gone, I might have met you even if we hadn't moved here."

When all that's left on our plates is crusts and I'm about to say I've got to get home, someone comes to the door. Coming back into the kitchen with a package, Hannah says, "It's from my dad. Probably for my birthday."

"Sorry. If I'd known it was your birthday— "

"It's okay, it was last month. But at least he remembered this year. Eventually."

Inside the padded envelope is a small box. Inside the box is a necklace.

"Nice," I say, even though I can't honestly see Hannah with a grinning Cheshire cat in neon colors hanging around her neck.

"It would be if I was still seven." She drops the necklace back in its box.

"Maybe he sent you money, too, or a gift card or something."

But all that's in the small envelope is a card with a bunch of bunnies on the front. Inside it says, '*Hoppy* Birthday. Here's *hopping* it's your best birthday ever.'

Hannah tosses it on her plate with the pizza crusts. "It's like he doesn't even *know* me."

"It sucks when your parents don't know you."

Hannah nods sadly.

"I've never heard you mention your dad – you know, any of the times you came over with your mom. I wasn't sure if he was even alive."

Hannah shrugs. "For how little I hear from him, he might as well not be." She starts picking little pieces off one of her pizza crusts and dropping them onto the plate. "He left when I was seven. I still remember it exactly. I was in my pajamas – pink with little teddy bears all over. I was playing with my Etch-A-Sketch on the coffee table in the living room before going to bed. I was making a picture of our house." Hannah takes her plate to the counter and stares out the kitchen window. "My dad came out of my parents' room with our heavy suitcase, the one we used when we went on holidays, and set it down by the front door."

This spilling-her-guts stuff is kind of embarrassing and I should be getting home, but you can't just say, 'I have to go get a prescription,' when someone's blurting out their life story. Besides, something about Hannah's tanned shoulder, turned my way now…

"Before I could ask him where we were going, he crouched down, kissed me, and said he loved me. Then he was gone. He never told me he wouldn't be coming back."

"Sorry," I mumble, blushing at the craziness of thinking I wouldn't mind kissing Hannah myself.

Again she shrugs. "It's not your fault my dad's a turd." She smiles at me then.

"If he's rotten enough," I say, "I could use him in my garden."

She looks at me with the same puzzled look I've seen when she's trying to figure out what Ivy is saying.

"You know. Rotten crap equals manure? Good for fertilizer?"

Hannah laughs. "You really are strange, David, you know that?"

"Yeah, I do."

Wishing I could stay, I get up from the table. "Sorry I have to go now, but I have to go to the mall for my parents."

"Okay if I come with you?"

Hannah *can't* come to the mall with us.

"Um...I have to take Ivy with me."

"So?"

Chapter 2

Hannah knows what Ivy looks like – her twisted arms and legs, her slightly too-big head, her eyes that sometimes cross, her saggy mouth – and she still wants to come. She's heard Ivy's grunting and shrieking at my place, too. But…

"Hannah, Ivy can be a real pain in the butt. Out in public especially. You know?"

"Come on, David. I like Ivy. Go get her."

I should just say, 'Forget it.' I know I should. But she actually wants to spend more time with *me*. So I can't.

Back home, my sister waves her hands and shouts, "Ga-beg!" – as close to my name as she's ever got. When she's this happy to see me, it's hard not to be sucked in.

I lean down so she can wrap her rubbery arms around

my neck and plant a slobbery kiss on my cheek. I rummage through the box by the door and call to anyone who might be listening, "Where's Ivy's sunhat?"

Dad steps out of his study into the hall. "Don't worry about it, David."

"She needs it," I argue. "It's hot out."

"You won't be outside for all that long. Just go."

"The mall's not exactly next door."

Dad sighs and goes back into his study.

I hate arguing, but at least I'm not invisible when we're arguing. I actually tried once to get into an argument with Dad on purpose. Knowing how he felt about the death penalty, I said I thought there were some situations when it should apply. He just shrugged and said, "Could be," like I wasn't even worth arguing with.

I find the missing sunhat on the coffee table under one of Mom's old gardening magazines. I'm tying the ribbons under Ivy's chin when she starts to shriek. I've tied them too tight and pinched her neck.

Oh well. It's not like she can report me.

I loosen the ribbons, wipe Ivy's drool off my hand onto my shorts, and wheel her down the ramp along the front of our house.

Hannah, coming down her driveway, has changed

into white shorts that really show off her tan and she's tied her hair up. Is it weird to be so taken by *shoulders*?

Ivy pats her head. "I ha?"

Hannah looks to me. "What did she say?"

It's cool that she cares enough to ask. Most people would just say 'That's nice' or pretend they haven't noticed she's spoken.

Ivy growls and yells, "I ha! I *ha!!*"

"She wants to know if you like her hat."

"I do!" Hannah answers. "I *do* like your hat!"

After walking a couple of blocks past an empty playground, Hannah says, "The mall's a long way to go for a prescription."

"Yeah, but the drugstore there is cheaper for some reason."

"It was really nice of your parents to invite me to your cottage so I don't have to go on that yoga retreat with my mom."

"They did?"

"They didn't tell you?"

"No."

"Would you rather I didn't come?"

"No! It's fine. I mean, I'm glad you can come." Bright sun reflects off the cars passing by on the busy street we turn onto. "You know, I never imagined that when Will, the old guy who used to live in your house, had to go into a seniors' home, that it would be someone like you who'd move in there."

"Someone like me?"

"Yeah. Someone who doesn't mind, you know, hanging out with me."

"Why would I mind? Are you a creep?"

"No. Just a geek."

Hannah laughs.

"You know what's funny? Whenever I went to visit Will, my parents thought it was nice of *me* to be keeping *him* company. They had no clue it worked both ways." We turn the corner past a church and a couple of banks. "Anyway, I'm glad you're coming to the cottage with us. Things have been a bit grim at our place lately."

"Oh?"

"Ivy's having another operation soon. My parents are kind of freaked about it."

"What's it for?"

"It's supposed to help with the seizures she's been having, but it also has something to do with the curve of her spine. That's been getting worse lately, and…" I stop. My sister starting to need diapers in the daytime again could be a bit of a gross-out. Not to mention embarrassing for Ivy. "Well, other stuff the doctors hope they can get her back on track with, too."

Stopping at a traffic light, Hannah says, "*Another* operation, you said? You make it sound like surgery's a regular deal."

"Regular enough."

On the other side of the wide intersection, three dog-walkers have stopped to chat. As we cross the street, Ivy shouts, "Dod bye!"

Again Hannah looks at me.

"Dog party. Like in *Go, Dog! Go!* It's Ivy's favorite book. She's crazy about dogs."

"She needs to meet my dog."

"Yeah, she'd like Shamus for sure."

About a block from the mall, three guys from school zoom past us on skateboards. One of them yells, "Hey, nice shorts, David."

Hannah glances down at what I'm wearing. I feel my bare knees blush nine shades of red. So I have no clue the right way to dress. But now that I think of it, I realize I've only ever seen the kind of shorts I'm wearing in gym class, which – as scrawny and klutzy as I am – I find as many excuses as I can to get out of.

Another guy says, "How's it going with your list of Greek words in alphabetical order?" Back in June he'd looked over my shoulder in the cafeteria when I was writing in my garden notebook.

So Hannah won't think I'm a total idiot, I tell him again, "It's not Greek. It's Latin plant names sorted by flower color and the seasons they bloom in. And I've never listed them alphabetically," I add. "What would be the point?"

It shouldn't be me who ends up sounding like a moron here, but of course that's how it goes.

"I don't know, David. You tell me. What would be the point?"

The third guy, checking out Hannah, says, "Nice girlfriend."

"We're just friends," I say. Are we even that?

"Oh right, *this* one's your girlfriend." The guy nods at Ivy, drooling and crossing her eyes. "The one with the pretty eyes."

"Bi-yee yies," Ivy says.

Another guy laughs. My hand clenches into a fist. Not that I could ever use it, but I wouldn't mind looking good to Hannah, standing up for my sister.

But beside me, Hannah giggles.

I give Ivy's wheelchair a firm shove forward – away from Hannah and down a curb. The wheels thunk down hard. "Damn you, Ivy," I mutter as we cross the parking lot toward the mall entrance. "I might have had a chance with Hannah if it weren't for you."

If a delivery truck were to come zipping along right now, I would gladly shove Ivy in front of it.

"David!" Hannah calls, scurrying to catch up. "I'm sorry. I just…I don't know…"

"Whatever." I've laughed along at wisecracks myself, stupidly hoping it would make me seem like less of a loser. *That kid's like a bad car wreck. Yeah, you know you shouldn't look but you can't help it. Haha-haha-ha.* "It's alright." And it is. Dad tells Ivy she's pretty all the time. She probably thought that guy back there was doing the same.

I give the automatic door opener a bash. With Hannah beside me, I push my sister inside where it's ten degrees cooler.

Chapter 3

On benches around the fountain, people escaping the heat are eating ice cream cones and slurping slushies. In front of a store having a big sale, Hannah spots a yellow top she likes.

"Why don't you go ahead to the drugstore while I try it on," she says, "and I'll catch up with you there?"

"It's okay. We can wait for you."

Careful not to block an aisle with Ivy's wheelchair, I stand off to the side of the entrance to the change rooms. While we're waiting, Ivy starts digging a finger up her nose. "Ivy, don't." I pull her hand away from her face. She growls at me and I can tell she's winding up to object big time if I try to stop her again. So the next time her finger disappears up her nose, I ignore it.

A minute later, "Yook!" A big, wet booger dangles from Ivy's finger.

I reach into my pocket for a Kleenex, but the woman handing out the numbered cards to customers who want a dressing room is on us.

"Don't you think your sister might be more comfortable over here?" She gestures to a corner out of sight of shoppers, where empty cartons have been tossed among the garbage bins.

If there's one thing I hate more than having Ivy make a fuss in public, it's having people act like a brain-damaged kid with cerebral palsy is less than human somehow.

I stare at her. "We're fine where we are. Thanks."

Hannah comes out of the change room, in the new top. "I think it might be too small," she says. "Do you think?"

It does this thing with her breasts that's different from any of the tops I've seen her in before. I feel my face go sixteen shades of red. "Um…" I use Ivy's wheelchair to hide the way the rest of me is reacting. "Yeah, maybe."

She goes back into the change room and when she comes out again, it's like those breasts have practically disappeared. She must wear one of those things girl runners wear – I've seen her jogging off down the street a few times. But I guess you don't wear one with a top like she just tried on. It's amazing what she can hide in that running bra thing. Seriously.

Since it's tough maneuvering the wheelchair in the narrow aisles of the drugstore, Hannah agrees to wait with Ivy on a bench nearby while I go in for the prescription. Waiting in line to pay, I can see her out in the mall, wiping drool from Ivy's chin. Then, saying something to Ivy that I can't hear, she circles my sister's face with her finger, then points to Ivy's eyes, her nose, and strokes her smiling lips. Could having a mom who works in pediatrics somehow make you immune to stuff like drool?

"Ga-beg!" My sister waves her hands excitedly when she sees me.

I ask Hannah, "Everything okay?"

"Yeah, fine. I was just teaching Ivy this rhyming thing I saw my mom do with one of her patients once. I think Ivy liked it."

Wow. This mall trip is working out way better than I thought it would.

Passing the fountain again on the way out, Ivy says, "Wah! Wah!"

"That was her first word," I tell Hannah. "Water."

"That's neat." Hannah smiles.

I turn Ivy so she can watch the water gush and tumble into the pool below the fountain. Right away, staring intently at the trickling streams and splashing droplets, she goes quiet. She better not have a seizure here. I mean, I'd know what to do and everything, but…

Hannah leans close to Ivy and says, "You like this fountain, don't you."

Ivy's head rolls to her shoulder. "Ngo waybo."

"No way? I thought you did."

More loudly, Ivy repeats, "Ngo *waybo!*"

Several people on the benches around the fountain turn their heads to see who's shouting, even the ones who've been trying to pretend they didn't notice her before. "Ivy, shh. Never mind." I have no clue what she's trying to say.

Loud enough for shoppers in stores halfway down the mall to hear, Ivy yells, "Ngo *waybo! Ngo waybo!!*"

If I could walk out right now and pretend I don't know the weird-looking kid bellowing at the top of her lungs, I would. As I grab the handles of her wheelchair to steer her out of there, Hannah calmly puts a hand on the back of my sister's head. "Ivy, are you saying, 'No rainbow'?"

Just like that, Ivy shuts up. Her grin fills half her face and she flaps her hands excitedly.

"Hannah, you're brilliant."

"What's it mean, though? No rainbow?"

"It means she noticed there aren't rainbows in the fountain water like there are in the sprinkler water at home."

Hannah couldn't look more impressed if Ivy was her own sister.

But she's my sister and sometimes, at times like this, that's okay.

Chapter 4

A wall of heat hits us when we leave the mall, but the sun has disappeared, thankfully, behind a cloud.

Back on our street, I watch Hannah head up her driveway. She turns and waves. Again I think of the breasts hidden somewhere under her shirt.

"Hey," she calls.

For a sec I think she's caught me checking her out.

"Does Ivy want to meet Shamus now?"

"Sure."

When Hannah opens the door, the dog bounds outside and runs circles around the front lawn. Ivy laughs.

"Want to see him do some tricks?" Hannah asks her.

Ivy waves her hands excitedly.

"Shamus, come." The dog trots over. "Shamus, sit."

Instead of sitting, Shamus lies down and rolls over. Ivy laughs.

Hannah says, "Shamus, take a bow." This time Shamus sits, and again Ivy laughs at his mistake. Hannah glances over at me and I'm not sure, but it's almost like it's me she's trying to impress. Wishful thinking?

"Shamus, can you *dance*?" Hannah holds a treat high above the dog's head. He stands on his back legs and turns around. Ivy waves her hands and squeals.

"Good dog!" Hannah says.

Shamus runs over to Ivy, sniffs her wheelchair, and lays his head in her lap.

Ivy tries to lean over to put her head on his but she can't quite reach. I wonder if she remembers our old dog, Livingston. Back when she could still walk with braces and canes, she used to lean on him to help her get around. A couple of years ago, when she was in hospital for one of her surgeries, my parents decided we had to have Livingston put down. We were having to support his rear end with a towel so he wouldn't fall over trying to do his business, and coming home to puddles of runny poop by the back door. I still thought it was cruel to have him put down. But when we all gathered around him on the vet's examining table – Mom, Dad, and me – we patted him and talked to him as the vet gave him the needle, and then he totally relaxed. It wasn't long till his breathing just stopped. I was surprised how peaceful it seemed. That's one of my few memories of us doing something together, just me and my parents.

Shamus leaves Ivy to go sniff a dog walking past. Hannah calls him back. "In the house," she tells him, and he trots up the steps.

Ivy and I head across the street. Near the start of the ramp that leads up to our front door, several sparrows fly out of a mock orange shrub. *Philadelphus coronarius.*

"Bi-yee fars. Eep, eep."

I wheel Ivy inside, park her by the living room window, and put her prescription on the kitchen table. Dad's putting finishing touches on a salad. The microwave beeps. From the back of the house Mom calls, "Davy, is that you?"

Piles of bills and receipts and stuff are spread across the desk in my parents' room. "Can you run outside and see if the last load on the line is dry?"

Ivy squeals from the living room, "Eep! Eep!"

Mom says, "I want to get it inside in case it rains tonight, but I need to sort out what's going on with this insurance. They seem to disallow something more every time we submit a claim."

"Sure."

"EEP EEP EEP!"

On my way outside, I ask Dad, "What's with Ivy?"

"EEEEP!"

Dad shakes his head. "Beats me. She seems to have a real thing about birds lately."

Chapter 5

It's different being with Ivy when it's just her and me, and when being with her is my choice, not my parents'.

Ivy pats the tummy of her turquoise bathing suit and beams. "Bi-yee bay zoot."

"That's right," I say. It's a conversation she wants to have at least six times whenever she wears it. "Your bathing suit is *very* pretty."

"*Ba-yee* bi-yee!"

Some days it's tedious but some, like today, it's kind of sweet.

I push Ivy in her outdoor wheelchair through the sprinkler in our backyard. When the spray hits her thin thighs and hunched shoulders, she squeals and waves her hands. At the far end of the patio, Dad's trying to fix the igniter on the barbecue. He says to Mom, "Have you ever seen a kid who loves water more than Ivy?"

Mom smiles. She's sewing up a tear in the cushion of Ivy's indoor wheelchair.

When my sister starts to cough, so suddenly and so hard she can hardly take a breath, I quickly steer her out from under the sprinkler and pound her back. My parents leap up and hover as if I don't know what to do. As if I haven't dealt with Ivy's coughing fits a hundred times before.

As soon as she catches her breath, Ivy cries out, "A-ghi, Ga-beg! A-ghi!"

"Again? Crazy kid."

Dad gives up on fixing the barbecue and Mom follows him into the house.

Again I push Ivy across the wet patio. As we make a turn, she looks up at me and grins. I bend down and kiss the top of her head. Halfway down the yard, a sparrow flies out of a tree.

After another few passes back and forth across the patio, Ivy goes quiet. Her hands, like claws, twitch on the arms of her wheelchair. Knowing what's coming, I steer her away from the sprinkler.

"Mom! Dad!"

Ivy's legs start jerking. Her head thrashes forward and back against the back of her wheelchair.

Mom rushes into the yard and grabs a towel from a lawn chair. Ivy's back is arched. Her arms and legs are still jerking. My stomach twists. Even though I wasn't cold a minute ago, I'm shivering now, my teeth clacking, my arms and legs juddering. I reach for my towel.

"*Three* seizures in the past *month*," Mom says.

For almost a year, she'd stopped having them at all.

Dad mutters, "Damn, useless medication."

"Stephen, don't start. Please."

They've been worse since they started up again.

Gradually Ivy's spasms become small twitches, and the twitches gradually come farther apart, until finally – finally – her rigid body goes soft. She looks around as if she doesn't know where she is. It's how she used to wake up from naps when she was little. Back then, Mom lifted her out of her crib and sometimes said, "Ivy, do you want to sit with your big brother for a while?" And she'd put Ivy on my lap and let me rock her till she was awake enough to want some juice or a piggyback ride.

Ivy still sleeps in a crib – a big one – and it's getting hard for Mom, or even me, to lift her out.

Dad takes Ivy from her wheelchair, holds her close even though she's soaking wet, and together my parents go into the house, leaving me to dry off the wheelchair and turn off the sprinkler. It bugs me that they've both gone inside without so much as a word to me. I mean, my stomach is still in knots, and it's not like it takes two people to put Ivy to bed, but it would never occur to them that her seizures might just freak me out.

But why *would* it? Unless they need me to do something, it's like I'm not even here.

Chapter 6

I chuck my towel onto the grass and go to the garage for string to tie up some delphiniums that have started flopping over the coreopsis in the front garden.

The plural of *delphinium* should probably be *delphinia*. According to a website I was on once, that's how 'um' words work in Latin. But even I'm not a big enough dweeb to call a group of them anything but delphiniums. I separate their tall blue stalks from the yellow daisylike coreopsis they're leaning on.

Today's seizure was a bad one. I wonder if we'll still get away to the cottage tomorrow. We better. Bad enough I couldn't go to music camp this summer.

Once I have the stalks all gathered together, I need an extra hand to wrap the string around them.

Three seizures in the past month, Mom said. No wonder Dad swore. I heave a deep sigh and glance up at the living room window where Ivy often sits watching me tend the garden, but of course she's napping now.

I lower the stalks gently and tie one end of the string to the railing.

She never had seizures at all before the surgery that went wrong when she was eight and I was twelve. Until then, she didn't need a wheelchair either. Back then, Dad used to do stuff with me. Like, he took me to the museum once and showed me stuff about ancient Greece – neat things they figured out about astronomy. And when we were at the cottage, he took me fishing. I remember once, we were sitting in a rowboat in the middle of the lake with the sun going down and the loons calling. We didn't catch any fish, but he told me the Latin name for the common loon that night. I still remember it: *Gavia immer*.

Again I gather the delphiniums close to the railing.

After today's seizure, there'll be more fooling around with Ivy's meds and more doctor appointments that both my parents will go to. A lot of guys would probably see that as a chance to raid the liquor cabinet or have a girl-friend over. But my parents can't afford to keep much in the liquor cabinet and I've never had a girlfriend.

The afternoon is hot. Heat bugs buzz above my head as I start tying the other end of the string to the ramp railing.

"David, hi."

I drop the flowers and stand up. "Hannah. I didn't hear you coming." I wipe my sweaty hands on my almost-dry trunks. "But you're here at just the right time to help me with this."

Hannah shoves her hair behind her ears. I never knew ears could be…I don't know…nice. She takes hold of the heavy stalks while I crouch down to tie the string.

"These blue flowers look great with the yellow dai-sies," she says. "Like sapphires and topazes all mixed together when the sun hits them."

It's neat that she noticed. That she sees it that way. But I hope she doesn't notice what she's doing to me, standing so close.

"It was kind of a happy accident," I tell her. "Nothing was blooming when I moved this coreopsis here. I just knew I needed something to fill a bare patch after a shrub died over the winter."

Still holding the stalks, Hannah says, "I saw you working out here so I came over to ask what time I should be ready tomorrow."

"I don't know. Nine? Ten?"

If we go. With Hannah coming with us, for five whole days, we *have* to go.

"Great." She smiles, and I almost drop the string.

Once the delphiniums are properly upright against the ramp, Hannah heads home and I head to the back yard. My parents are talking quietly on the patio, looking like they'd rather not be interrupted.

Slipping away, I hear Mom say, "No, Stephen, absolutely not. I've said it once and I'll say it again. I will not send our daughter to live in a group home. Her home is here, with us."

Wow. I've had moments of wishing Ivy out of my life. Sure. But to actually send her away? To live with strangers? Not that anyone's asking me what I think, but that's just nuts.

Chapter 7

When I cross the street to tell Hannah we're just about ready to leave for the cottage, Shamus again greets me with his stuffed monkey hanging from his mouth. From upstairs Hannah calls down to me, "Come on in. I haven't quite finished packing."

I go in, give Shamus a pat, and call back, "Don't forget your bathing suit." I just mean so she can swim. I hope she doesn't think I meant so I can see her in it.

For the first part of the trip, Hannah and I take turns playing on my Gameboy, an old one I picked up at a consignment shop. Strapped into the van's middle seat, between us and my parents, Ivy squawks and burbles. We stop for lunch on the way up, a packed picnic because of how hard it is with Ivy in a restaurant. Then we drive on for another hour.

The closer we get, the more nervous I get. I mean, Hannah's only coming to our cottage because her mom knew my mom, but still...

Hannah says to me, "It's far, isn't it."

We turn off the paved country road onto a gravel one.

"Yeah, but we're almost there now. Another ten minutes."

Passing the acres of dunes that separate the road from the lake just before we get to our place, I tell her, "It was right about here that Livingston always started whining to get out of the car. He loved it here."

By the time I've explained who Livingston was, we've made it down the long, narrow laneway that passes through a wooded area and leads to our cottage. Overlooking the water, it's a small prefab that Dad inherited from his parents. The only work he's done on it, or had someone else do, is building a makeshift ramp and widening the inside doorways. It's pretty rustic.

Mom puts Ivy down for a nap while the rest of us unpack the van. When the groceries are all put away and suitcases are unpacked in the bedrooms, Hannah stretches out with a magazine in the hammock strung up between a pair of birch trees. Her long, athletic legs look even longer when she's not standing or sitting. If she knew how I've started thinking of her, would she mind?

Not far from the hammock, Dad's raking twigs out of the beach sand while Mom is inside making the beds. I wander over to the hammock and set it swaying. "Do you want to go for a walk?"

"Arf, arf!"

"I didn't mean it like that. There are some neat dunes not far along the shore I thought you might like to see."

Neat dunes. It sounds lame, even to me.

Hannah fans herself with her magazine. "Maybe tomorrow, if it's not as hot?"

"There's rain forecast tomorrow," I tell her.

Hannah shrugs. "I'll take that chance. Is that okay?"

Can she tell that showing her the dunes was just an excuse to get her alone somewhere?

I head into the cottage for a drink. Dad puts away his rake and follows me inside. Hannah, close behind, sits down on the couch and picks up my Gameboy. I hand her a can of pop from the fridge.

"Thanks."

After a while, a sound like a siren comes from Ivy's room.

"Stephen, can you go?" Mom's hands are in the sink.

Dad carries Ivy, rubbing her eyes, into the living room. A stunned expression flashes briefly across Hannah's face. I can't figure why at first. Then I realize. In the three weeks she's known us, she's only ever seen Ivy fully dressed. Looking at my sister through Hannah's eyes, I see what I hardly think about anymore – the delicate white curve of Ivy's back, her sorry little legs.

And the diaper. Getting up from her nap on the hottest day of the summer, that's all she's wearing.

"David, spread a blanket on the floor, would you?" Dad says. "Ivy'll be cooler there than in her wheelchair."

Hannah jumps up to spread out Ivy's blanket and sits back down beside me. She's watching closely as Dad lays Ivy gently on the floor and kneels beside her.

"Did you have a good sleep, sweetheart?" he says. "You missed the baseball game on the radio. The Blue Jays won it in the ninth inning."

"Eep eep? Fabel cow boo."

Hannah is still staring at them, so I nudge her elbow. "Are you going to play with that Gameboy, or what?"

Without taking her eyes off them, she hands it to

me. "The way your dad talks to Ivy and she makes those sing-songy sounds back at him? It's so nice. Like they're having a real conversation."

Ivy reaches up and pats Dad's chin.

"Want to get up, darling?" He cups the back of Ivy's head and lifts her off the floor.

Ivy pats his back. "Da-a da-a."

Hannah's face goes all mushy and for a second I think she's falling for my dad, which is really gross if you think about it, but then she says quietly to me, "I wonder if my dad ever held *me* like that. I'd remember, wouldn't I?"

Dad puts Ivy in her wheelchair and turns it so she can look out the window. "There you go, sweetheart." When he leaves Ivy and goes into the kitchen, Hannah's eyes follow him.

After lunch we all get into our swimsuits and head outside. Hannah's is a red two-piece. I quickly wade into the water up to my waist. Ivy pats her turquoise tummy as Dad carries her into the lake.

"Bi-yee bay zoot."

"That's right," Mom says. "Your bathing suit is very pretty."

"*Ba-yee* bi-yee!"

From the shore, Hannah watches Dad swish Ivy

back and forth in the water. When he pauses, Ivy shouts, "A-ghi!" and Hannah smiles.

Mom laughs and calls across the water, "She wants more, Stephen."

"I know. But she's heavy. She's not a little girl anymore." Half laughing, he flips Ivy onto her back. Her hair makes a swirling halo in the water around her head as she stares up at the sky, with Dad's hands underneath her. I wade through the water toward them.

"Here, Dad, let me." I take Ivy and swirl her back and forth through the water. Her hands grip the backs of my arms and her face is one wide-open grin. I swirl her suddenly in the opposite direction and she laughs so hard she's soon got all of us laughing – me, Dad, Mom, and Hannah still up by the shore, looking gorgeous in her red bathing suit, burying her feet in the sand at the water's edge.

After a while my parents take Ivy inside. "How about a swim?" I suggest to Hannah.

"Promise you won't think I'm an idiot?" she says.

"Why?"

"David, promise?"

"Okay, I promise I won't think you're an idiot."

"I can't swim."

"Well, let me teach you then."

"No, seriously. Please? I can't."

She looks so panic-struck, I just say, "Sure. No problem."

That evening during a rummy game, the heat breaks. A cool breeze blows in the window. My parents take turns playing hands so one of them can be with Ivy, trying to figure out how to calm her down. She's been wailing pretty steadily ever since we finished '*feemeen*' but I hardly notice because under the table, Hannah's foot is leaning against mine. She probably doesn't know she's doing it. She probably thinks she's leaning her foot against the pedestal in the middle of the table. But all I care about is the pressure of that bare foot nestled up against mine in the dark space under the table.

Chapter 8

After a night interrupted a few times by Ivy hollering, I wake to the sound of pounding rain on the roof of the cottage. Over breakfast it settles into a steady drizzle, the kind not likely to let up any time soon. So much for walking in the dunes with Hannah today.

After breakfast, she pulls a thousand-piece jigsaw puzzle from a shelf, an old one Mom got years ago, when she was the one into gardening. Together, Hannah and I clear the table to make room for it and start sifting through the box for edge pieces.

Most of the edge and the hydrangeas in the lower half of the puzzle are together, we've eaten lunch and the dishes have been cleared away, and still the rain continues.

Mom's busy with Ivy, Dad heads into the kitchen to try to fix a leaky pipe under the sink, and Hannah and I go back to our puzzle. With her shoulder so close beside mine, it's easy for me to imagine she feels the same about being close to me as I feel about being close to her. And there's that ear that I can't not look at every time she tucks her hair behind it.

Into the sound of the wet clattering on the roof comes the tinkly tune from a jack-in-the-box that was Dad's when he was a kid. *All a-round the cob-ble-er's bench, the monkey chased the wea-sel...* I played with it too, back when I was my parents' only kid.

Mom sings along with the tinny music coming from the box. "The monkey thought it was a-all in fun..."

Of course I lost interest in the toy long before I was eleven.

"What comes next, Ivy?" Mom asks.

The rain clatters on. I look up from my search for a lopsided H-shaped piece of red peony and see Ivy lift her head from her shoulder as if she's about to answer, but her eyes aren't focused anywhere, and her head flops again toward her chest.

Mom turns the handle again. Jack jumps out of his box. "Pop!" Mom says.

WHAT HAPPENED TO IVY

Still Ivy doesn't react.

Mom finishes the song and begins cranking the handle again. Again the tinkly tune, and again, "All a-round the cob-ble-er's bench, the monkey chased the wea-sel... The monkey thought it was a-all in fun..."

Sometimes Ivy yells 'pop' before it's even close to time for Jack to jump out of the box, but today Mom waits, again. Again she says, "Pop!" and again finishes the song. Along with the tinkly tune, she again starts to sing, "All a-round the cob-ble-er's bench..."

Dad pulls his head out from under the kitchen sink. "Give it up, Anne. Can't you see she's never going to get it?"

"Yes she will. She's got it before. Lots of times." Mom keeps turning the handle. "The monkey chased the—"

"*Stop!*" Dad clenches the wrench tightly in his fist. "*Look* at her! She doesn't have a *clue* what you're going on about!"

I glance at Hannah. She's either doing a good job of pretending she doesn't notice the tension or else she doesn't think my parents arguing is any big deal.

"Sometimes she just needs more time," Mom says.

Suddenly I get a whiff of something I hoped wouldn't happen when Hannah was around. Hoped! I practically *prayed!* Not that I'm religious. It's just that I've had enough friends who came over after school once, and that was it, because of some gross thing Ivy did. And it doesn't get much grosser than filling your pants.

Hannah's face says she's caught it now, too. Burying her nose in the crook of her elbow, she whispers, "Pwah. That's worse than a Shamus fart."

In the kitchen, Dad throws down his wrench. "Shit!"

Hannah jumps. We both do.

"Stephen!"

Dad tears his jacket from the hook beside the door and storms out into the rain.

Chapter 9

Lifting Ivy from her wheelchair, Mom winces. She better not put her back out. No way I want to get stuck hauling my sister around in her shitty diaper.

After Mom takes Ivy into the bedroom and closes the door, I open my mouth to apologize, but Hannah just shakes her head. "It's okay, David. No big deal." She leans across me and fits in a piece that finishes the peony in my corner of the puzzle. "Really."

I take a piece of baby's breath from the box and try it near the red peony. It doesn't fit.

"Try it over here," Hannah says.

I lean across her to reach the section of puzzle with fine white flowers in it – *Gypsophila paniculata* – and place the piece in the space she suggested. Her neck smells of gardenias. Could I kiss her now, while my parents and Ivy are all somewhere else? Would she let me? What if I just—?

Mom comes out of the bedroom and sighs. Having put Ivy down for a nap, she puts a kettle on for tea.

An hour later, when the tea's all been drunk and the puzzle's well over halfway done, a cool damp breeze sweeps in the back door. Dad shakes the rain from his jacket and hangs it up. Rubbing the space between his shoulders, Mom says, "Look at you, Stephen, your jeans are soaked." As if he hadn't noticed. I guess it's her way of apologizing for pushing it with the jack-in-the-box.

After he's changed into dry clothes, Dad carries Ivy into the living room and lays her on the floor. Sitting on either side of her, my parents bend and straighten her legs, moving them as if she were riding a bike. Ivy grimaces and groans the whole time.

"That looks painful," Hannah says.

Dad says, "It is."

I'm so used to the physio that someone has to do with Ivy several times a day that I forgot Hannah's never been around to see it. Bending and straightening Ivy's left leg, Mom says, "Ivy puts up with a lot, but we have to do this to keep her spine from getting any worse before the surgery, and so she doesn't lose muscle tone."

When Ivy's back in her wheelchair, Dad props up a felt board and starts sticking fuzzy animal shapes on it. Pointing at a duck, he says, "What sound does a duck make, Ivy?"

Nothing.

"A duck says, 'Quack quack.' Ivy, can you say, 'Quack quack'?"

"Buh buh buh."

"Christ, why do we bother?" Dad stuffs a handful of felt animals back into their box. "Honestly, Anne! Why do we bother with any of it?"

Hannah glances up at me. Mom is definitely giving the onion she's chopping way more knife than she needs to. Even I'm surprised by how testy Dad is today. If it wasn't raining so hard, Hannah and I could go somewhere else.

When the felt board and animals are back on the shelf, Dad sighs.

"It's alright, Ivy. Who cares what a duck says anyway, right?" He lifts her out of her wheelchair and starts dancing her around the cottage. He sings, "I'd do anything for you, dear, anything…" Cradled in his arms, Ivy coos. "For you mean everything to me."

When he puts Ivy back in her wheelchair, Hannah goes over and runs her finger around Ivy's face. "The moon is round as round can be." Wouldn't I just love to have her trace my face with her finger like that. "Two eyes, a nose, and a mouth, I see."

"Boy, this puzzle is really coming along, isn't it." Dad's standing behind me.

"Yeah, this section here was pretty hard. Now I'm just trying to figure out where this—"

Ivy shrieks. It's a piercing shriek and Dad is by her side in a shot.

I chuck the piece that I'm now showing to no one onto the table.

So, big deal Dad was actually showing an interest in what I was doing. So, big deal it didn't last because Ivy needed something. When *doesn't* she need something? When isn't she messing up *something*?

Like when I was in grade six and had my first solo part in the school concert. My parents actually found someone to stay with Ivy so they could come. And didn't I sing my heart out that night. *I would not be just a nothin', My head all full of stuffin', My heart all full of pain, Perhaps*

I'd deserve you, And be even worthy erve you… But it turned out they weren't there to hear me because between the time I went to the school to get into my scarecrow costume and make-up and when they were supposed to get there, Ivy got a fever that spiked so high they had to rush her to hospital. I wished that night that she'd never come out.

Chapter 10

During supper, it finally stops raining. As Mom dishes out strawberries for dessert, Dad suggests having a bonfire. "Or would people rather just play a board game?"

Hannah accepts a bowl of berries. "Do you have Monopoly?"

This cottage thing is turning out okay. I mean, it could have been that Hannah would think stuff like puzzles and Monopoly were totally dorky.

Ivy waves her hands. "Haw! Haw! Haw!"

"Let's have a fire," Mom says. "Ivy does love a fire."

"Sure." I hold out my bowl for extra berries. "Let's do what Ivy wants for a change. We hardly ever do what Ivy wants."

Dad gives me a look.

After supper, it takes several tries to get the damp newspaper lit, but once the flames take hold of the kindling, the fire gets going pretty quickly. Somewhere far off, an owl hoots. Ivy hoots too.

Mom brings out a bag of marshmallows, Dad gathers a bunch of sticks, and I spread a tarp over a damp log for me and Hannah to sit on.

I watch her ram a marshmallow onto her stick and twirl it over the flames. When it's roasted crispy brown on the outside and all gooey inside, I watch her pull it off the stick and put it in her mouth. I touch my chin to tell her she got a bit of melted marshmallow on her chin. She wipes it off with her finger and pokes it into her mouth, staring at me full on the whole time. Sitting on that log, our thighs are touching, and she knows I'm not a table leg this time.

I'm just pulling a third marshmallow off my stick, thinking maybe I'll feed this one to Hannah and imagining what her lips on my finger would feel like, when she jumps up and shouts, "What's wrong!? Something's happening!" She drops her marshmallow into the fire.

Ivy is convulsing – harder than I've ever seen. Her back arches, throwing her head hard against the back of her wheelchair. Her eyes roll up and disappear into her head and her whole body keeps on jerking – hard, and harder still. It's like she's being electrocuted.

Sounding extremely calm, Mom says, "It's okay, Ivy, you're okay. We love you, darling, and we're here."

Tears stream down Hannah's face. Dad looks like he could cry, too. I can practically feel the juddering all up and down my own arms and back.

Mom's voice keeps on, low and even, "It's alright, Ivy. It's going to be okay."

Gradually the convulsions loosen their grip. Blood trickles from the corner of Ivy's mouth. Finally, after what feels like ages, she slumps over in her chair, limp.

Wiping tears off her face, Hannah asks, "Is she okay?"

Mom says, "She will be."

How? How can Ivy ever be okay?

Dad breaks his marshmallow stick and tosses it on the fire.

"Hannah," I ask, wiping blood off Ivy's lip with my sleeve, "are *you* okay?"

She nods but her face is pale.

Dad lifts Ivy from her wheelchair and carries her into the cottage, her arms and legs limp, her head hanging limp against his shoulder. As they pass through the door, Mom reaches up to stroke Ivy's limp hair.

It's just me and Hannah outside now, with the flames crackling and the moon shining overhead. But all I can do is douse the fire.

Out on the lake, a loon cries.

Chapter 11

The sun's shining when I wake up and I can hear Ivy banging on the jack-in-the-box and yelling, "Bop! Mucky fuh. Bop!" It seems she's no worse off for last night's seizure.

Maybe today I can persuade Hannah to come with me to the dunes.

I get up, get dressed, brush my teeth and head into the living room. "Where's Hannah?" I ask.

Mom says, "She went for a run up toward the highway."

"Bop! Mucky fuh. Bop!"

"I didn't think she could be sleeping through that."

I get the *Encyclopedia of Perennials* from my room and

look up plants that flower in the fall that might be good in my garden, adding them to the list in my notebook.

Eupatorium because the mauve would look good behind the dark green mugho pine.

"Eeep! Eeep! Eeep! EEEP!"

The birds again.

Caryopteris because it's gray-green leaves look good even when it's not blooming.

"Kreeeeeee!"

Helianthus because it attracts butterflies and birds.

"Aw-aawwk!! A-awk! Kree, kreeeee!!"

Forget *Helianthus*.

Hannah glistens all over when she gets back from her run.

"Kreee!"

She gulps down a gallon of water, then hits the shower.

"A-awk a-a-awk! Eeep! Eeep!"

After Hannah has breakfast, she takes her magazine out to the hammock. I close the encyclopedia and my notebook and wander outside.

"Are Ivy's bird calls getting to you, too?" I ask.

Hannah shrugs. "A bit."

"We could go for a walk," I suggest.

"Good idea." Hannah follows me inside to get her sandals.

Dad is marking his students' essays. Mom is washing out Ivy's clothes that got messed yesterday.

"We're going for a walk," I tell them. "Me and Hannah."

"Oh, can you pick up some eggs, David?" Mom asks. "I forgot to put them in the cooler when I packed it. We could use some more bread, too."

"Kreee, kreeeeee! A-awk!!"

There's no point arguing. No point saying the store isn't where I was planning to go. At least she can't make me take Ivy because the gravel road would bung up her wheels. Still, I can't get us out of there fast enough. Hannah is right behind me as I push open the screen door. Suddenly it's quiet, then—

"Baba, Ga-beg. Baba, Hahn."

Hannah stops. "Hey, did you hear that? She said my name! Hahn – that's me! I didn't know she even knew my name. Did you, David?"

On some days I might be impressed, but today Ivy's too under my skin for me to care. "Let's go."

Hannah runs over and kisses my sister on the fore-head. "Bye-bye, Ivy."

Away from the cottage, it's so quiet. Dodging puddles, Hannah and I stroll along the road.

"I finally got an email from Casey," Hannah says, "just before we came up here."

"Who's Casey?"

"A friend from my old neighborhood who's been away on holidays since before Mom and I moved here. Well, not here. To our new house. Where your old friend used to live."

I won't ask if 'Casey' is a girl or a guy. Instead I ask, "When school starts up, will you be going to Meadowview?"

"Yeah, in grade ten. Is that where you go?"

"Yeah."

"What are the teachers like?"

"Well, you don't want Doyle for English. He assigns way more essays than Barclay."

"I wouldn't mind that."

"Hanley's the best, if you'll be taking Music."

"It was my best subject at my old school. I was in stage band and the choir."

"I'm in choir, too," I tell her. The way she just nods I can't help feeling like some over-eager puppy trying to please its person.

By the time we get to the store, the sun has dried the wildflowers growing in the ditches at the side of the road. We get the bread and eggs and I pick up a couple of packages of candy, too. Licorice twists for me and Hannah, and gummy bears for Ivy.

On the way back to the cottage, I swing the bag of candy at my side. Carrying the eggs and bread, Hannah says, "The blue of those flowers in the ditch reminds me of the flowers we were tying up a few days ago."

"Yeah. The delphiniums."

"And what are these?"

"Cornflowers. They're nice with the Queen Anne's lace here, aren't they?"

"Maybe you should plant some Queen Anne's lace with your delphiniums," Hannah says.

"I think it's a weed, isn't it?"

"You're asking me?" Hannah smiles. It's like she knows what a geek I am and doesn't care. Maybe she even likes it. And even though a cloud is casting a shadow across the road, I feel like the sun has never shone brighter.

I'd move the bag of candy to my other hand and take hold of Hannah's, except the bag has made mine all sweaty. Okay, so that's lame. So, I'm chicken and I'll probably die wondering if I ever had a chance with her.

"Want to drop off our stuff and walk some more?" Hannah suggests.

Is grass green? Is the sky blue?

Just as we're about to turn down the dirt track toward the cottage, I hear a vehicle coming along the road toward us. White. Lights on top.

An ambulance.

Hannah and I keep to the side of the road to let it pass.

It doesn't. It turns down the dirt track to the cottage.

Ivy.

Hannah drops her bag.

Crack!

And we run.

Chapter 12

A paramedic is kneeling on the ground at Ivy's head. Her wet hair is splayed out across the sand. An oxygen mask attached to some kind of squishy balloon thing covers much of her face. Dad, in wet trunks, paces the sandy shore, clutching his arms to his chest, his jaw moving as if he's shivering badly or else talking to himself. Mom looks paralyzed, standing to one side and clenching the phone in her fist. Another paramedic presses down on Ivy's chest, rhythmically and hard. I almost yell, 'Not so hard, you'll hurt her.'

But now the paramedics are lifting Ivy onto a stretcher. Her skin doesn't seem pink enough, but she'll be alright. Won't she?

Dad stares at the ambulance as it pulls away, his mouth hanging open. His eyes are dark hollows in his face. Gulls hang in the air above the shore.

For a moment everything has stopped. There's no sound, no movement. It feels like there's no air to breathe.

Then Mom rushes toward Dad.

"Stephen, let's go!" When he doesn't move, Mom grabs him by the arm and yells, "I'll drive." He stumbles with her to the van, mumbling something about a seizure. Hannah and I still haven't moved.

I can hear the wheels of the ambulance crunching onto the gravel road and the van following. The lake laps the shore as if nothing has happened.

What *has* happened?

Hannah and I went to the store.

We strolled back along the gravel road with bread and eggs and licorice twists and gummy bears. And now... Is Ivy...?

I'm still clutching the bag of candy I bought.

I can eat it all myself now.

Stupid!

I fling the bag to the ground. *Stupid!!*

I charge into the lake, bashing the water with my

arms. It's heavy against my thighs. I hurl myself forward and start kicking.

My clothes are leaden. I thrash through the water till my lungs ache.

A voice on shore calls my name. "David!"

It sounds far away. I don't care. I keep on swimming, farther and farther out. In my ears the buzz of a motor-boat bee-lines down the lake. And in my chest, wanting to explode.

I roll onto my back, gasping. I float. Like a dead man. I float until my lungs stop burning. I fill them with air and I start making my way back to shore.

When I get there, Ivy will grin. She will shout my name, 'Ga-beg!' And together we will eat licorice twists and gummy bears.

My legs tremble as I plod through the shallow water close to shore. Stepping onto the beach, I stub my toe on a rock. Water streams from my shorts and t-shirt. The hot sand burns my feet. I've lost my shoes in the lake.

Hannah staggers toward me. "You idiot!" she cries. "Didn't you hear me calling you? I thought you were going to drown, too! What were you doing? You *idiot!!*"

I trudge past her and into the cottage. I wanted to be with her. If I hadn't wanted to be with her, none of this might have happened. If we hadn't gone to the store…if we'd hurried back…if we had all been here…maybe…I can't think any more.

I change into dry clothes and stay in my room until I hear the van.

In the living room, Hannah is sitting tightly curled in a chair in the corner, biting the ends of her fingers. She looks up at me. "Sorry I went kind of hysterical on you."

As if that's what matters now.

When the screen door opens, I turn. Despite Dad's tan, his face is white. His trunks are dry now. Mom's eyes are puffy and red.

Together, my parents sit down carefully on the couch, like they're visiting someone else's home.

"So…?" I can hear that my voice is hollow and tight.

Dad says, "Ivy kept going on about the birds. The whole time I was marking my papers. But I was determined to get them done. I didn't want them hanging over me the whole holiday."

"Who cares about your damn papers? What's happened to Ivy?"

Dad gets up and turns to leave the room.

"Davy…"

"Somebody just *say* it!" I can't control the anger or the tears now.

Dad goes to the window, staring out. "She's gone," he says. He doesn't look at me.

I look at Mom as if she might tell me something different. But she just wraps her arms across her stomach and rocks forward to stare at her feet.

"She had another seizure," Dad says.

"Even worse than the others," Mom adds.

"You were there, too?"

"No, I was lying down inside. I heard your dad yell. He said, 'Ivy's in trouble. Call 911.'"

It feels like we're talking about whether to order take-out chicken or pizza, not how my sister died.

"The stupid thing is," Dad says, "I didn't even realize that's what was happening. Not right away…It was just… while I was holding her…" He holds his arms out the way he holds them under Ivy when she's floating on her back. The way I've seen him do it dozens of times. "This look came over her face. Suddenly." He shakes his head, like he still can't believe what's happened. "I looked up to see what she was looking at…"

"Gulls," I say.

Dad turns from the window. "What?"

"Gulls. I saw them, too."

Like it matters what I saw. Like anything matters now except that Ivy…

Dad's face crumples.

I can hardly make out what Mom says next, she's talking so fast and crying so hard. "I ran outside and there she was…limp, she was just limp and now she's gone, but I can't believe…she can't be, she was just…she was just *limp*."

I can't look at Dad or Mom. And I can't look at Hannah either. All I can do is stare at the blood oozing out the end of my toe. Because today? Today *I* couldn't wait to get away from my sister. My sister. Who's gone. And this time she *isn't* coming back.

Chapter 13

No one talked in the van on the way home. Hannah went to her place as soon as we got back.

Now Mom and Dad are making arrangements for Ivy's funeral. They've called the funeral home. And they're meeting with a minister about the service.

I think one of the songs should be "How Much Is That Doggy In The Window" or "When You Wish Upon A Star" because they were Ivy's favorites, but no one is asking what I think.

I click through pictures on a horticulture website on the computer in the family room without really looking at them.

I'd go see Hannah, to be with her, but I wanted to be with her and not Ivy, and now that I can't ever be with Ivy again, how can I be with Hannah?

Chapter 14

The death notice my parents put in the paper is small. Beside a tiny picture it says: Ivy Jasmine Burke, daughter of Stephen and Anne, sister of David. It gives her date of birth, the date she drowned, and the time and place of her funeral. Turns out the seizure isn't what killed her. The autopsy report said it was the water she took into her lungs when she had the seizure.

The next day, the paper prints a tiny article saying a child with severe disabilities drowned while in the water with her dad. Filling the rest of the page is news about the death toll from heat waves across the US having risen to more than a hundred. It takes up lots of space, like the story about a little girl whose body was found under some bushes last year. She'd been abducted on her way home from school, raped, and beaten.

Those are the things people care about. Lots of people dying in huge natural disasters and cute little kids dying gruesomely. Not the death of a not-so-little girl so severely disabled it was hard for most people to even look at her.

I keep thinking we're going to get a call from the hospital any minute to tell us we can come get Ivy and bring her home. I want to make her laugh again. I even want to wipe her slobbery chin.

But then, with Ivy gone, maybe Dad and I can go fishing again. Maybe next time I have a concert, he and mom will get to it. If they can get a babysi—.

They won't need a sitter.

It's impossible to stay inside, thinking, thinking, thinking all my stupid thoughts.

On my way down the ramp into the garden, I pause and grip the railing. Ivy was cooped up in the house a lot. She'll never ride down this ramp again. The wood of the railing under the midday sun is almost hot enough to burn my palms. I wish it was hotter.

Kneeling in the garden, I can't figure out what to do with myself. I keep thinking of Dad and Ivy in the water.

How he had her on her back, and she was looking up at the sky. And I wonder, when the seizure started and Ivy's back arched and the water covered her face, did she feel the water going into her lungs? Did she struggle? Is that why Dad couldn't get her out of the water in time? Because she was struggling and convulsing and hard to hold?

I look up at the window where Ivy should be watching me, then stab my trowel into the ground. An earthworm wriggles into the dirt.

Mom said when she saw Dad carrying Ivy to shore, she was limp. I try to replay again what must have happened, and what it must have been like for Ivy while Hannah and I were walking along that road. God, I was so *happy* then! While my sister was *dying*, I was *happy!*

But damn! Is it a crime to want to be happy?!

Ivy would have been happy looking up at those gulls. *Aawk! Kreee!* Maybe they were the last thing she saw, looking up through the water while Dad held her.

Maybe she didn't struggle.

Still, I can't settle down. Not even in the garden. I'd go talk to Hannah, I can't *not* talk to Hannah, but she took off for a run a while ago and I haven't seen her come back.

Later that night, finally drifting off to sleep, I hear someone calling. I pull my pillow over my head, my whole body heavy with exhaustion. Again, this time loud enough to hear – "Ga-beg!"

I sit up. From the bathroom across the hall comes giggling and the sound of water splashing.

"Ga-beg, tum tee!"

I have woken from a long nightmare. Ivy is not dead. She's alive and laughing in her bath!

I throw off my covers and hurry across the dark hall. It's dark in the bathroom, too. Of course. And silent. The whole house is as silent as a tomb.

Chapter 15

The day of Ivy's funeral is overcast, but hot enough that by the time we get to the church my shirt is sticking to my back. My parents and I wait in a small room until just before the service starts. Filing into the church itself, I can see that the pews are filled with people, but not who they are.

The minister strides in, his long robe fluttering around his ankles. He clears his throat. "Let us pray." On either side of me, my parents bow their heads politely. I bow my head, too. My shirt collar chafes my neck.

How did I ever think having my parents all to myself would be a good thing? Because I never imagined sitting between them in a church, the air muggy and thick with the stink of lilies and gladioli, around a coffin with my sister inside it, that's how. Riding bikes to the botanical gardens together, maybe, or traveling to see the ancient sites that Dad lectures about at the university. Not like this.

"Amen."

The minister raises his eyes to the rafters and launches into his sermon.

"We are – all of us – God's children. And so, He chooses when our time on Earth shall begin, and when it shall end. Some He leaves on Earth for a long time before calling them to His side, and some – like Ivy Burke – for only a short time."

Yeah right. And what if *God's children* would rather stay with their *real* families?

"God has His reasons for choosing those He does, when He does, unbeknownst to us though these reasons may be. It is a privilege, nonetheless, to be chosen, or to have a loved one chosen."

What a crock. And *unbeknownst*? What century is this guy from anyway? My parents used to go to this church, years ago, but it must have been a different minister then. This one's got nothing to say about Ivy that he wouldn't say about any other dead person. She was much loved. She was a fine person. She will be missed. And there's more yammering on about 'a better place' and 'life everlasting' and blah, blah, blah, until finally the service ends and anyone who'd like to 'pay respects to the family' is invited back to the house after the burial.

On the way out of church, I see Hannah and her mom. The little boy I babysit every Tuesday night is here, too, with his mom. I wonder if Will came, if he saw the notice in the paper. Would someone from the seniors' home have brought him? I haven't seen him.

At the cemetery, the minister does an 'ashes to ashes, dust to dust' thing and throws a handful of earth down onto the lid of Ivy's coffin. *Ka-thunk.* "Dear Lord," he says, "may Ivy Jasmine Burke rest in peace."

It's a nice idea: Ivy hanging out with the angels, free of all the crap life handed her. Too bad I can't buy it.

Trying to make small talk over stupid little sandwiches back at the house is even worse than the service. Neighbors, friends of my parents, and distant relatives who haven't seen me in years, if ever, either look at me with a creepy mix of curiosity and pity, or else blab on about stupid things as if it doesn't really matter that Ivy is dead. Snatches of conversation barely register in my brain.

"You can get them way cheaper at Costco."

"They'll be staying with us right through to the end of the summer."

"It's all re-runs now. I never watch it anymore."

Ladies from the church pass trays of disgusting crustless sandwiches full of pickles and mayonnaise and bright red cherries. The bitter smell of coffee in the urn in the kitchen mixed with the sickly sweet smell of the sandwiches practically makes me gag, especially when a fat guy with a mountain of them heaped on his tiny paper plate starts talking with his mouth full. And people thought Ivy was gross.

When I turn away, a neighbor from down the street is standing at my elbow. "I'm so sorry, David," she says. "This will be hard on your parents, losing a daughter." Across the room, my parents are standing shoulder to shoulder, nodding their heads as words of sympathy drip from the mouth of some neighbor who always looked away when I passed her on the street with Ivy. They feel tight, my parents, like they always do – together in a way that doesn't include me.

I'd like to say to the neighbor from down the street, 'Losing a sister is no picnic either.' Instead I nod politely and say, "Excuse me. I need to get something to drink."

On the way to the kitchen, I pass Murray, the kid I

babysit, sitting in the hall with a book about trucks across his lap. His mom, Tina, is in the kitchen, washing up a few dishes. "This is so sad, David. I'm so sorry."

"Thanks."

Tina takes her hands out of the sink and dries them on a towel crumpled on the counter. "Listen, David, I know you said before you went to the cottage that you could take care of Murray tomorrow afternoon while I paint our front door, but if you'd rather not, I certainly understand. The door can wait."

The whole scene here – the people, the formal clothes, the small talk, the fake food – feels totally unreal. "No, I'd like to. It'll feel sort of, I don't know…normal. You know?"

Murray's mom nods sympathetically, which is almost harder to take than people who don't understand, so I head back to the dining room.

I hoped Hannah would come over after the funeral, but I haven't seen her. An old guy with a kind face is standing alone, looking at a display of photos that my parents must have thrown together sometime since we got home. For a sec I think it's Will. But it's not.

Two gaudy bouquets flank the photo display. It includes stuff like Ivy grinning broadly on Santa's knee and Dad holding Ivy up on Livingston's back so she can ride him like a horse. Ivy gazing at bubbles I'm blowing for her in the backyard. There's one of Ivy trying to blow out the seven candles on her birthday cake, too. I always ended up blowing out her candles for her, right up to her last birthday. She should have had more than eleven.

Talking to the old guy might be better than standing around like a piece of furniture. But it doesn't matter. He's moving toward the front door now. He's leaving. Good idea.

I'm dying to yell through the crowded rooms, 'Would you all just hurry up with your stinking little sandwiches and go home!' and see everyone scramble for the door like ants when someone disturbs their hill.

But no. The torture continues.

"I hear your Lucas is off to university in the fall."

"I wonder if Anne will go back to work now."

"It must be reassuring to know their little girl is at peace."

That 'peace' idea again. As if anyone can *know* that dead people are at peace. Maybe dead people are just that. Dead. And maybe there's no right thing for people to say when someone dies, just a hundred wrong things.

A woman I don't know, someone Dad works with

maybe, walks up to me and smiles. "Really, it must be a *relief*, in a way."

Make that a hundred and one. I hate the woman's too-bright lipstick and the smudges of make-up on the side of her neck.

And I hate that she is right.

"We loved her," I say. "And you've got something green stuck in your teeth."

Across the crowded room, someone laughs. I have to get out of here. When I turn, I see Hannah over by the stairs to the side door. She's changed out of her funeral clothes into a light shirt and pants. Her mom says something to her and Hannah nods. When her mom leaves her, Hannah looks right at me. Her eyes are blue and sad and beautiful and I have to be with her.

I tip my head toward the hall. We slip through clots of people and disappear into Ivy's room.

Chapter 16

Ivy's pajamas are still hanging over the dropped railing of her crib. Her pink blanket lies in a heap where it landed the last time someone got her up, before we went to the cottage. As we stand there together, being with Ivy's things, Hannah knows somehow not to say anything. It's nice.

The little nubs on Ivy's blanket are soft under the tips of my fingers. With anyone else, I'd be embarrassed to lift it to my face, but for some reason with Hannah it's okay.

The blanket smells of baby powder. In one of the pictures on the board in the dining room, I'm holding Ivy wrapped in this same blanket. I was almost four and she was a tiny infant. Mom had one arm around my shoulder and with the other she was making sure Ivy didn't fall off my lap. But Ivy was *my* little sister, and was I proud.

I remember the feel of her arms around my neck, later, when I was old enough to go to school. The slobbery kisses she planted on me every day when I left. And the way she shrieked '*Ga-beg!*' whenever I came home. Remembering is like a stab in the gut. Remembering the nice things but also remembering how I pretended she was nothing but a big pain whenever other kids were around.

Thing is, she *was* a big pain sometimes. Lots of times. Including the last time I saw her alive. I never knew missing someone could actually *hurt*.

"What are you thinking?" Hannah asks.

"I don't know."

After a while, only a few quiet voices drift in from the living room, along with the sounds of someone rinsing dishes and loading the dishwasher. Fiddling with a sleeve of Ivy's pajamas, Hannah asks, "Do you believe in heaven?"

I set Ivy's blanket back in her crib. "No. Do you?"

She shrugs. "I think so. But not with angels and stuff."

"What then?"

"I don't know. I think heaven might be different kinds of places for different people."

It's hard to see how that could be possible, but I won't argue. Not with Hannah. Instead I reach up and wind Ivy's mobile.

Its colored fish swim in circles to the tune of "When You Wish Upon A Star," quickly at first, then slowing. I tell Hannah, "This always helped Ivy fall asleep, even on her bad days. Sometimes we had to wind it up twice, but hardly ever more than that."

Hannah bites down on her lower lip.

Each slowing note plinks out a memory of Hannah doing something with Ivy: reading to her at the cottage. Doing 'the moon is round as round can be' around her grinning face. Holding a sprig of lavender up to Ivy's nose for a sniff. That was the first time Hannah came over to our house with her mom, the day after they moved in.

My arm brushes against hers. Her skin is warm and soft. I'm aware of the flowery smell of the shampoo she uses, the soft sound of her breath, and the row of tiny buttons down the front of her shirt. A tear slides down Hannah's cheek to the edge of her mouth. With my thumb I wipe it away. And then, just lightly, I kiss her.

Her lips are salty and wet and how is it I've waited so

long to do this? Having tasted her I can't stop wanting to taste more but that's okay because – oh God – Hannah is grabbing my head. She is kissing me back. My tongue finds the hot inside of her mouth and—

As suddenly as it started, she shoves me away. "I have to go."

Swiping the back of her hand across her mouth, she leaves me then, shaking and alone, beside Ivy's crib.

Chapter 17

Going to bed that night, I know I've blown it. I can't stop the brain-loop replaying that kiss and how it went wrong, and somehow that woman who somehow knew I'm relieved that Ivy is gone keeps getting all mixed up in it.

I should never have kissed Hannah. What was I thinking?

I *wasn't* thinking. But the kiss wasn't a problem at first. Because Hannah kissed me *back*, I know she did. And who *wouldn't* be relieved that life might finally not be *all* about someone who was always messing things up, anymore? Besides, it's not like relief is the *only* thing I feel.

I've just turned off my light when the phone rings.

My parents don't seem to be answering. The jangling this late at night sets my teeth on edge. Why hasn't the answering system kicked in?

I haul myself out of bed and grab it. Unknown Caller. "Hello?"

"Hey. Are you the guy who killed his own kid? You deserve to die." *Click.*

Chapter 18

Tina opens her tin of paint. It's a deep red like the cardinal flowers in my front garden. "Nice color," I say.

"Thanks." Tina shoves a cap over her loose curls. "It's really good of you to be willing to take Murray off my hands for a while, what with…everything."

At the playground, I let Murray play in the sandbox way longer than it takes to paint a door, then push him on the swing for a while. On the way home, we stop at the variety store. Before we go in, I give Murray a few coins to spend on whatever he wants.

"Can I have gummy bears?" he asks.

I lean heavily against the brick wall to catch my breath.

"What's the matter?" Murray asks.

I try to come up with some excuse for why I'm suddenly falling apart, but I hate how people always avoid telling kids the truth, so I swallow the lump in my throat and make myself answer him. "I was just thinking about my sister."

"Oh." Murray examines his coins. "Your daddy maybe drownded her because she lived in a wheelchair, right?"

"What!? Who told you that?"

"Mrs. Meyers at the pet food store told it to my mom when we were buying budgie food."

"Well, Mrs. Meyers is *wrong*, okay?"

First that creep – the one who called – went from reading, 'disabled kid drowned,' to 'her dad must have done it.' Now Mrs. Meyers is assuming the same thing. And how many people has *she* talked to? How many other people are talking like that about what happened to Ivy?

We go inside so Murray can buy his candy.

Sitting on the grass outside the store, he holds out his package and says, "Do you want a gummy bear, David?"

"No, thanks."

I lie back on the grass, watching clouds scud past overhead while Murray nibbles the head off each bear before eating the rest of it. I remember hearing once about some guy who offed his kid by gassing her in his pickup truck. But he must have been off his nut. Dad *couldn't* have done what Mrs. Meyers said.

When Murray has finished his gummy bears, we get up and start toward our street. I'll have to tell Hannah that if her mom buys dog food at Mrs. Meyer's store, she should start getting it someplace else. Except I can't. I can't talk to Hannah about anything now. Why didn't I just keep my stupid feelings for her to myself? It was bad enough kissing her when I didn't even know if she liked me, but to go and do it right after Ivy's funeral? Right there in Ivy's room? And I couldn't just make it a nice little kiss either. I had to go and practically ram my stupid tongue down her throat. I never would have done that if Ivy hadn't gone and died, that's for sure. Even dead she's messing things up.

When we get back to Murray's, the paint on the front door is dry. Tina tries to pay me for the extra time we were away, but I tell her it's okay, today was a free one.

Back home, rather than going inside, I grab a trowel from the garage. I jab it into the ground in the front garden, hoping Hannah might come out of her house while I'm out here. I dig out an ugly weed, bash the dry earth from its roots, and drop it into a bucket. I dig out another weed and then another.

Ivy loved everything in the garden. Even the weeds. 'Mmm, bi-yee fars,' she said again and again, 'Bi-yee fars.'

There was so much more to her than most people knew. Like Mrs. Meyers, for one. And I should have told Murray that Ivy wasn't just a girl in a wheelchair. She was also a girl who liked flowers and birds, and she liked gummy bears, too, just like he does. I should have told him that on good days she liked pushing Jack back in his box so someone would turn the knob and make him jump out again. And that she liked bonfires and roasted marshmallows and listening to stories, the same stories he likes, and that her favorite was *Go, Dog! Go!*

I should have told him how Ivy loved water – in the bathtub, the sprinkler, her therapy pool – and how she knew that sprinkler water has rainbows in it but not the fountain at the mall, and probably not the lake where her dad took her swimming, either. I should have told Murray that Ivy probably saw things in the lake that ordinary people like us couldn't see, but no one would ever know for sure because she couldn't talk very well, and sometimes that made her mad. I should have told him that if Ivy could talk and if she were still alive, she'd want to tell

Mrs. Meyers, and anyone else like her, that her dad didn't drown her. Because he couldn't. He loved her.

I dump the full bucket of weeds onto the compost heap in the back yard and go back out front to dig up some more.

I loved Ivy, too. But I bet she didn't know it. Besides all the times I didn't speak up for her – like today, which was nothing compared to sometimes – there were the times I did worse than not speak up for her.

Like the time I got invited to a friend's birthday party, back when I still got invited to things like that. It was going to be a great party, a trip to a circus. Except at the last minute Ivy started throwing up and convulsing and when I said it was time to drive me to the party, my parents wouldn't listen. I was so mad I went and dug worms out of the garden and I fed them to Ivy, knowing she could never tell. I'd never done anything crueler than pinch her before that, and that was when she was a baby and I was just little. But I was ten when I fed her the worms. Old enough to know that what I was doing was cruel and disgusting and downright *wrong*. But it didn't matter. I took a worm, placed it on Ivy's tongue, and watched her squish it all around and swallow it – and then I fed her another.

I sit back on my heels. Hannah still hasn't come out of her house and I don't want her to now. It feels like if she did, she'd see worm guilt tattooed all over my neck and down my arms.

Chapter 19

I wake to the sound of Dad's voice in the kitchen.

"...strangest thing, Anne. I keep thinking that when I was carrying Ivy to shore, something moved. Up in the dunes."

"Some animal, you mean?"

"No. Like someone was standing there watching, and then quickly ducked down."

"That's hardly likely, Stephen. There's no one along our stretch of shore but us."

"I know."

"And besides, if someone *was* there, surely they would have come over to see if they could help."

"You're right," Dad says. "Of course. I must have been mistaken. There can't have been anyone there."

"Stephen, are you alright? I was about to go out for a while."

"Yeah, fine. I'm fine. Go."

It's such a bizarre conversation I might wonder if I'm dreaming. But the pressure on my bladder is real-world. So is the clinking and clanking of dishes being taken out of the dishwasher and the sound of the van starting up and backing down the driveway.

After taking a leak and splashing water on my face, I head out to my garden.

Just beyond the wheelchair ramp, is a single, odd-looking plant that's beautiful in a weird way. This spring it had both dark red flowers and cream-colored flowers on it. I went online to see if I could find a scientific explanation for how that could have happened, but nothing explained it very well.

It has a few new buds on it today. I sprinkle fertilizer around its base, the kind that encourages flowering. Then I refill the bird feeder. I can't stop myself from looking up at the window, half-expecting to see Ivy watching me. I pull a few dried leaves from the stalk of the odd plant.

Often, when Ivy used to watch me out here, I felt a neat bond with her. Today it feels broken. I try to imagine her face at the window, but I can't see it. Ivy's *face*! How can a guy forget his own sister's face?

I glance across the street as if Hannah might be heading over to see me. She's not.

I suppose she might forgive me, some day, for that stupid, oafish kiss. But I need Ivy to forgive me, too, for stuff I did to her. And that can't happen. I look up again at the empty window. I can't feel her here at all. Not like I did last week, standing beside her crib, listening to her mobile, with the baby powder smell of her still clinging to her blanket.

I put the rest of the birdseed in the garage and head inside, hoping to get Ivy back, at least for long enough to tell her I'm sorry. I wash the earth from the garden off my hands and head to Ivy's room. When I reach the doorway, I stop.

Where my sister's crib used to be, where it should be, where it has always been, clumps of dust waft across the hardwood floor.

Heavy footsteps trudge up the stairs from the basement. Dad looks surprised to see me. Has he forgotten I exist? That I live here, too?

I shove my words in his face. "Where's Ivy's crib?" As if it's not obvious he's taken it apart and stashed it downstairs somewhere.

"In the basement," Dad says, as if that's a perfectly logical place for it.

"Well, what if…?" My voice is too high, but I can't help it. "What if I wanted to hear Ivy's mobile again? Eh? What if I did?!"

"*What*? Hear her *mobile*?" Dad throws up his hands, lets them drop, and shoves past me. "Honestly, David, sometimes I wonder about you."

"*Me*? You wonder about *me*? Who's the one trying to make like Ivy never even existed!? Did you even talk to Mom before you did it?! Did you?!"

Dad stops and turns. "Excuse me?" He shakes his head. "I don't have to answer to you," and he storms back downstairs.

I jab my thumbnail into the soft wood of the door-frame on my way to the family room and mutter, "Yeah, tell me about it." The van pulls up the driveway.

After Mom puts away the groceries, Dad comes up from the basement. He tells her about Ivy's crib and apologizes for taking it down without talking to her about it first.

"Oh, Stephen," she says, starting to cry again. She turns away and empties a can of soup into a pot.

Sitting down with Dad, she says, "Come on, Davy. Come have some lunch."

I glance at Dad. "I'm not hungry," I say.

Chapter 20

That night at supper, none of us is speaking. The clinking of cutlery on our plates sounds amplified. Even chewing and swallowing sound loud. Mom asks for the butter. It seems Dad didn't hear her, so I take some myself, pass it to her, and go back to pushing vegetables around my plate. The bread is stale and the potatoes aren't hot enough to melt the butter.

From across the table comes a sudden spluttering, like someone's choking. Dad raises a napkin to his face. I jump up from the table. I know the Heimlich maneuver. I can be Dad's hero.

But he's not choking. Mom has cried plenty in the days since Ivy died, but not like Dad is sobbing now.

She puts a hand on his arm. "Stephen, what is it?"

It's embarrassing is what it is.

Dad shakes his head, his mouth moving the same way it did when he was pacing the shore after the ambulance left. "I started to lift her," he finally says. "As soon as I saw that Ivy was in trouble, I started to lift her."

"Of course you did." Mom's voice is calm, reassuring.

"I *started* to…"

My fingers clench around my fork. Mom wipes her lips with her napkin.

"You see, Anne…" Dad's voice has gone high like mine does when I'm upset. "She looked so…*happy*. Just before the seizure. Ivy…well…" All the color has drained from Dad's face. He clears his throat. "It occurred to me…"

Oh God.

"Well…I…" He covers his face with his hands. He breathes into his palms like someone who can't get enough oxygen.

"Stephen, please don't do this."

Yes. Stop. Now.

Dad drops his hands to his lap. Lines of anguish etch his face and I can't look at him.

"There was just a second…I swear…when Ivy's pain…and I thought…"

"You can't have thought…" Mom's voice is slow and quiet, as if something will break if she doesn't speak carefully.

"I thought…No I didn't, but I…you know…our marriage. Just a second or two."

Just a second or two what?

"Stephen…"

"David, too."

Is he trying to say…? He started to lift her, then for a second or two…Pins and needles shoot through my arms to the tips of my fingers. Ivy was limp, Dad said, when he carried her out of the water.

But she goes rigid during a seizure. That's why her head went under the water. My heart pounds. Whatever Dad thought, or whatever the hell he did, it wasn't for just a second or two.

My knees bounce up and down under the table and I can't stop them.

Dad speaks quietly, so quietly I can barely hear. "I let her go, Anne."

His words are like a punch in the gut. And I've taken too many. Starting with the sound of eggs cracking. When I knew it was the sound of death, but not that death wouldn't be the worst thing. I race to the can. I puke.

Later, I burrow into my bed. He let her go. He could have saved her and he didn't. My dad took Ivy in the water and he let her *die* there! And *I've* felt bad about feeding her a few lousy *worms*!?

Through the wall I hear change from Dad's pocket dropping onto the dresser. My parents haven't spoken since supper. I hear a short, single creak of their bed followed by footsteps in the hall and someone settling in on the couch.

I guess they'll split up now. I mean, their kid is dead because Dad decided that would be okay. Mom couldn't possibly stay with him knowing that, could she? So they'll have to split up, won't they?

I don't even care.

Chapter 21

Mom's eyes are puffy when she asks me to go pick up a sleep remedy she got the pharmacist to set aside. I'm glad for the excuse to get out.

There's no one around on the streets or in the playground beside the school. Despite the strong wind, it's too hot for most people. But I spot Hannah running along the street between the new video store and the vet clinic. She's been running more often since Ivy died. Since the day I kissed her, over a week ago now.

At the mall, flags are flapping straight out from their poles. I lock up my bike. A few guys from school are hanging around the entrance, but they just look at me. I guess making fun of the guy whose sister died would be going too far.

I head right to the drugstore. As the pharmacist hands over Mom's package, she says, "I was sorry to hear about your sister. If you're having trouble sleeping, you can use that remedy, too, if you want. It's perfectly safe."

I soon find myself parked on a bench by the fountain, staring into the spray. Ivy was right. There is 'ngo waybo' here. I hear a snippet of conversation from the other end of the bench.

"But is it wrong to kill a kid if she's suffering and you know her life's never going to get any better?"

All anybody knows for sure is that Ivy died. No one knows what Dad admitted to last night. Maybe whoever is at the other end of the bench isn't even talking about Dad. Ivy's life wasn't that bad.

"...seriously, what's the point of a life like that Ivy kid's anyway?"

I open my mouth to tell them. It won't be like it was with Murray this time. But while I'm still struggling to find the words I need, they get up to leave – two people I recognize from last year's History class. They're disappearing quickly down the mall. Standing up, I shout at their backs, "Letting someone go and killing them – it's not the same."

Shit! That's not what I meant to say!

They turn around and look at me like I'm some kind of freak, and they're not the only ones.

I pedal across the bridge over the highway, past the road to the cemetery, past motels and car dealerships, and beyond the edge of the city to where old barns and farmers' fields line the road.

No one knew how Ivy died before I opened my big mouth. What was I doing defending Dad anyway? *If* that's what I was doing. Whatever people want to say about him – he deserves it. I ride for another hour, maybe more, hot sun and wind blasting me before I turn back.

Sweat trickles down my forehead and into my eyes. When I come to the road to the cemetery, I turn down it and ride on through the gates.

Someone else is already at Ivy's gravesite. It's Dad, standing with his back to me. I should have noticed our van parked on the edge of the road nearby.

I turn around and start pedaling hard. I stand on my pedals to get my speed up so I can get out of the cemetery before Dad sees me. Because what if he didn't just let her go? What if he actually drowned her? And what if he didn't just decide to do it right then, when he had her in the water and her seizure started?

Leaning into my handlebars I pedal as hard as I can out of the cemetery. Did Dad know when he took Ivy in the water that day that she was going to die there? Is that what he meant by the bonfire, when he kept telling her, 'It's okay, Ivy, it's going to be okay'? Or was it Mom who said that? Maybe it was Mom.

My left calf cramps in a painful knot. Still, I keep on pedaling. My thighs burn and all I can see in front of me are Dad's big brown hands and Ivy's turquoise bathing suit under the water. My legs start to wobble, my hands are trembling on the handle-grips.

Be-ee-ee-eep! A passing car swerves around me. I crash into the curb and go down.

My elbow and the side of my leg sting. They are scraped raw and full of gravel. They sting so bad my whole body sweats and my head spins. But I pull myself up, and then my bike. Leaning on it, I hobble along the shoulder of the road. After a couple of blocks, our van pulls over just ahead of me.

Dad lifts my bike into the back, slams the door, and gets in beside me.

"Where have you been?" He eases back into the traffic. "You've been gone for hours."

"Nowhere."

"We were starting to worry."

I could ask him now. I could ask him: *Did you drown her? Did you plan it, like I planned the worms? Did you know when you helped her into her bathing suit – her 'bi-yee bay zoot' – what you were going to do? Or not till you carried her into the water and made her laugh one last time?*

But do I really want to know?

Chapter 22

I hand Dad the sleep stuff that Mom wanted and go knock on Hannah's door. She has to be back from her run by now and I've got to see her.

Shamus barks but no one else comes to the door. I cup my hands around my eyes and peer in the narrow window beside the door. Shamus grins and wags his tail.

At home I clean up my scrapes and try to lose myself in a search for info about plants that should grow well in our area. Maybe Hannah's not avoiding me, maybe she's just been busy.

Eupatoriadelphus maculatus.

I have to talk to her.

Parthenocissus tricuspidata.

But what if I've totally messed things up with her for good?

I shut down the computer, turn on the TV, and click mindlessly past soap operas and talk shows and dozens of ads. There's nothing on that I want to watch. I cross the street and knock on the door again. This time Hannah opens it.

"Are you okay?" she says. "You look awful. Do you want to come in?"

"You don't mind? After…"

Stupid of me to refer to it. It was days ago and she asked me in, didn't she?

Hannah shrugs and tucks a loose strand of hair behind her ear. "People do weird things after someone dies."

Is that what it was to her? Me kissing her? Her kissing me back? *A weird thing*? So, what was I expecting? For it to mean 'true love' and 'happily ever after'?

"Hannah, I have to tell you something." She's walking down the hall so I follow her to the kitchen at the back of the house.

"What?"

"My dad…well…At supper last night…he kind of broke down…"

"That's hardly surprising, David. He's lost his little girl."

"Yeah, but…"

From across the kitchen Hannah is staring at me like I'm nuts, and maybe I am. But having to talk to someone, not even knowing what I want to say – and Hannah's arms are crossed and she's leaning back against the counter and maybe she *is* still ticked – there's like this war going on inside me. Do I want to tell her about Dad or just about my stupid outburst at the mall? But why tell that? She already thinks I'm an idiot, and telling her that would be like telling her everything anyway.

"Hannah, Dad didn't just lose Ivy."

I should stop now. This was a bad idea. I should just take myself out of Hannah's kitchen and forget the whole thing.

"He let her go."

Hannah shakes her head. "Go where?"

Suddenly weak, I lean back against the fridge. "He let her *go*, Hannah. He took Ivy swimming…and when she started having her seizure he started lifting her…out of the water." My bones have turned to jelly and I slide down the fridge to the floor. "But then he didn't."

Hannah turns away and shoves her hands into a sink full of dishwater. "Don't be ridiculous."

"He admitted it, Hannah. Last night. He said it to Mom…He said, 'I let her go.'"

"You're lying." Hannah's words are tight. Her shoulders are hunched up tight around her ears.

It sounds crazy even to me, but my gut reminds me it's true. The tears are starting now. Shamus saunters over, flops down beside me, and lays his head across my lap.

"Hannah, listen. I wish I *was* lying. I don't want to be right about this…But I thought…"

I don't know what I thought.

Hannah spins away from the sink and grabs a dish towel. "*You* listen, David." She glares down at me from across the room. "I have watched your dad with Ivy and he is a *great dad*. Do you know how *lucky* you are, having a dad like him? How can you expect me to believe such a…such a *lie*?"

Hannah hurls the dish towel and it hits me in the face. I manage to rise from my spot on the floor and charge out of the house.

Chapter 23

An electric current is buzzing through me. I try to cry for help...But my chest...Something heavy...I sink deeper.

Gasping for air, I wake, tangled in my sheets. I rip myself free of the bedding and fill my lungs again and again.

Hannah didn't believe me and I didn't even get to the worst. That maybe Dad didn't just let Ivy go, maybe he made her go. Because maybe he got fed up. Fed up like I got fed up. Fed up with all her shrieking like a dozen damn birds, and with all her shitty diapers. With having to hold her down every single time she had to take her meds, and fed up with all her 'special needs.' Then when he's doing something that's supposed to be so straightforward and pleasant – fun even – she goes and has another damn seizure. And suddenly he sees this chance to stop it. All of it. For good.

I turn over my pillow but even its cool side is hot.

Looking at just the facts of what happened – forget *how* it happened – it's actually no wonder Mrs. Meyers and others came to the conclusion they did. A man takes a helpless, severely disabled kid into the water – a kid prone to seizures who can't even walk, never mind swim – at an isolated cottage where no one will see them. His son isn't around, his wife is napping, and the next thing anybody knows, the disabled kid comes out of the water dead.

But if anyone who mattered thought that, like cops and stuff, wouldn't they have reported it? And if Dad was right about someone in the dunes seeing him with Ivy that day, they'd have gone to the cops, wouldn't they? If they saw him doing something wrong?

I think too much. All this thinking has my guts in a mess. A bowl of cereal might help settle things down.

A faint light from the kitchen is shining into the hall. Whichever of my parents went to bed last must have forgotten to turn it off.

No. Mom is in the kitchen in her bathrobe, pushing

an iron back and forth across the sleeve of one of Dad's shirts.

"What are you doing?" I ask her.

The iron hisses steam. "I couldn't sleep."

I could say, 'Dad's the one who should be having trouble sleeping, he's the guilty one.' But I don't. "Me either," I say, "but I don't want to iron."

Unless…could Mom be feeling guilty, too?

She turns over the sleeve. "What do you want, David?"

My thoughts are so confused I'm not even making sense to myself anymore. "Something to eat." I get a bowl and cereal from the cupboard, milk from the fridge, and a spoon from the drawer.

Is Mom awake, trying to figure out how to leave Dad? Ironing his shirts so he'll have some to wear for a while after she's gone? She keeps ironing the same, already smooth shirt. She looks even more tired than she did when Ivy was alive. But no one would iron shirts for someone they were leaving. Besides, now that I think of it, neither of my parents headed to the couch after they got ready for bed earlier.

I chew on a mouthful of cereal until it's a dry lump in my mouth and force myself to swallow. Mom keeps pushing the iron up and down the same sleeve of Dad's shirt. Up and down again. I dip my spoon back into my bowl.

"Dad really loved Ivy," I say. "Didn't he." Not a question.

Mom looks up. Startled. As if she's just remembered I'm there. "Of course he did. We all did."

Yeah, we all did. But that didn't stop me feeding her worms. It didn't stop me pushing games with her too far. Like the time I was dragging her around the house by her feet and she thought it was really funny, so then I started pulling her down the stairs because I thought that would be even funnier. But she stopped laughing pretty fast because every time her head hit another step, it bounced. *Thunk. Thunk.* All the way to the bottom.

I wipe a dribble of milk from my chin.

"Listen, David." Mom switches to the other sleeve of Dad's shirt. "I know having Ivy for a sister wasn't always easy for you."

How much does she know, I wonder? Did she know before, or not till after Ivy was gone?

"What Dad did…" My spoon carves aisles through the cereal in my bowl. "How are you…? How can you…? Well, it seems like you're okay with it. I mean—"

"You mean what Dad *said* he did?"

"Well, yeah."

"David, your father…That night…Your father didn't know what he was saying. He was – he *is* – simply grief-stricken. And he feels guilty. He thinks he should have been able to save Ivy that day. That's all. Your dad…" Mom rests the iron on its base. "He didn't do what he said. He could *never* have done what he said."

I cling to my spoon as if that will somehow make it true, what she is saying.

"You know, David, he's been having nightmares every night since Ivy died. Every night. Last night at dinner, when he said the things he did, he was just confusing his nightmares with what really happened."

She sounds so convinced. But she *has* to believe what she's said. She couldn't stay married to Dad if she didn't. And I guess she needs him. I don't.

"Okay?" Mom says.

The whole scene, dimly lit by the light above the stove, feels surreal. Mom hangs Dad's shirt on the back of a chair. It looks very white, whiter than it does in the daytime. She sets the iron on the counter and packs up the ironing board.

"Yeah."

"You'll get back to bed soon, then?"

"Sure."

Before I finish my cereal – I should have just dumped it and gone back to bed when Mom did – Dad trudges into the kitchen.

"Your mother said you were awake." He pours cold coffee into a mug and sits down across from me.

The last of my cereal floats soggily in my bowl. At the edge of my vision, I can see Dad's hands wrapped around his mug. The hands that used to support Ivy in the water. The hands that should have saved her when she got into trouble. I feel his eyes staring at me.

"She would have been having surgery today," he says.

The clock on the stove says it's three o'clock.

"I'll tell you now, your mother and I were terrified."

I was always at school when Ivy was having surgery. I could never focus on what any of the teachers were saying. Half the time it seemed as if the hands of the clock had all but stopped moving.

"We didn't tell you this before because we didn't want you to worry, but the surgeon was going to have to expose her spinal cord."

A bead of sweat trickles down the small of my back.

"It was a pretty risky procedure," Dad says, "with no guarantee it would work."

"So, why are you telling me now?"

"I'm sorry. Maybe it was a bad call."

"Yeah, maybe." I get up to leave but Dad goes on talking.

"The time they had to adjust the shunt to keep fluid from building up in her brain – that was supposed to be routine…"

I feel like I'm in some weird kind of waking nightmare. First Mom, convinced that Dad didn't do what he said. Now Dad – what's he doing? Trying to justify it?

I wish he would just shut up.

"Remember," he says, "how Ivy used to lean on Livingston to help her walk when she was little? And how sometimes she fell asleep on the floor with him?"

I remember. I remember Ivy clutching Livingston's coat and nuzzling her face into it, too. At least if Dad has to keep on talking, he has changed the subject.

"Of course, you were devastated when we had to have him put down."

My jaw tightens. "In case you didn't notice…" My fists are clenched now. "*Ivy* wasn't a *dog*. She was my *sister*! And you…you had *no right*…"

Dad sets down his mug. "Who did then, David? *You?*" He folds his hands as if it's either that or hit me. "Tell me. Did *you* sit through hours of medical consultations with teams of doctors with fancy solutions to Ivy's problems but no sense of what her life was like? Did *you* sit up with her in the night while she cried and you could almost never figure out why, and even when you could you couldn't do anything about it? Did *you* have to try to reassure her a hundred times a week that it was going to be okay, knowing it wasn't? Eh, David? Did you?"

I hate him more than I would ever have thought possible. "It was her life. Hers to decide what to do with. Not yours."

Dad looks at me like I'm the biggest fool living. "Ivy wasn't capable of that kind of decision and you know it." He's breathing hard. I can feel him hating me as much as I hate him. And stupid as this is, it occurs to me that he's paying attention to me and no one's interrupting, and isn't that what I wanted? What I thought I wanted?

Now that I've got it, it couldn't feel worse.

"David, listen to me. Please." Dad pushes aside his mug. "I'm as upset that Ivy is gone as you are. I'll dare say I'm *more* upset because she came from me and because *I* had that moment when I could have…" Dad gets up from the table and looks out the window into the dark night. "I loved her, David…What else can I say? I loved her."

I know he did. It's in his voice. It's in the haunted face I can see reflected in the dark window. I also know that I could stay here for a long time on the slim chance Dad might eventually get around to saying he loves me, too.

I get up from the table, dump the rest of my soggy cereal down the sink, and stagger back to bed.

Chapter 24

Despite how little I've slept, I'm awake early, which is good. I can get out of the house before my parents are up. I stumble to the kitchen for a glass of orange juice, then go stand in the empty space by the living room window.

A sparrow scrabbles pointlessly at the feeder that I've only thought to fill once since Ivy died. Two more peck at the ground underneath it. She sometimes drove me nuts talking away to the damn birds, but geez, what I wouldn't give now for the chance to hear her 'eep'ing and 'awk'ing and 'kree'ing again.

I miss Ivy and I miss Hannah, too. I even miss old Will who used to live across the street. I gulp down the last of my juice, set the glass on the windowsill, and head down Ivy's ramp to the front garden. I pull some dead flowers off their stems and drop them to the ground.

Last night, was Dad trying to say he did what he did because he loved Ivy? How is that supposed to make sense? I'd sure never try to claim I fed her those worms because I loved her.

In my hand is something soft. I look down. The crushed, blood-red cardinal flower in my fist wasn't ready to be plucked. *Lobelia cardinalis*. I gather the dead blossoms from the ground and take them to the compost bin in the backyard. It works better if there's garden stuff mixed in with stuff from the kitchen.

The compost bin is almost full. What's in the bottom of it, crawling with earthworms, is ready to be used.

Removing it with a shovel, I breathe in the moist decaying smell of it, then take it out front and spread it over the ground between some shrubs. I dig it in with my hands, crumbling it together with the dry earth. I do it slowly. It takes a long time.

It's quiet here in the garden. I love how the sun warms my back and the top of my head, how the light shines through petals and leaves creating multiple shades of green, pink, yellow, and blue. I love how all of it helps me stop thinking.

At a flash of movement in my peripheral vision, I glance up.

Rushing toward me is Hannah. Every inch of her skin is glistening. Strands of sweaty hair stick to her face. She hurls herself to her knees beside me, practically collapsing against me.

"I needed him to be better," she cries. "I thought he was perfect."

The back of Hannah's shirt is damp beneath my hands. She smells like summer even though she's been running.

"But you wouldn't lie to me, David. Why would you? I just…" She wipes her face across my shirt. "I just didn't want to have to believe you."

Chapter 25

All I can do is hold her. She doesn't try to say anything more and I can't speak at all. What is there to say now, anyway? *I'm sorry. I'm sorry, too.* Hannah's breathing gradually returns to normal and she eases herself away from me.

"I have to go," she says, standing up and brushing dirt off her knees.

As she's crossing the street to go home, I can see I've left grubby handprints on the back of her shirt. My shirt's still damp from where she was leaning against me.

There's nothing left for me to do in the garden right now, so I hop on my bike, ride out to the nursery and talk to a guy there about delivering some mulch. On the way home, signs at the mall shout 'Back to School Blowout Specials'. Hard as it is to imagine being back at school, I'm going to need paper and pens and stuff, so I go inside.

Parents are hauling kids from one store to another shopping for new shoes and backpacks, and going for fries and slushies. A couple of girls I'm sure never noticed me while Ivy was alive eye me from behind a rack of sweaters, whispering behind their hands. As I'm passing the fountain, a little kid breaks free of her dad's grip and wobbles toward it. He scoops her up and flies her through the air back into her stroller.

I load up on paper and pens and binders at the department store and realize I won't be able to carry everything on my bike without my backpack, so I put everything back on the shelves and leave.

Pedaling up our street, something doesn't look right. Closer to home I can see that the purple phlox near the sidewalk is all bent over. A small mound of mugho pine has been flattened. I see as I ride closer that a long board is lying haphazardly across them both.

Up near the house, Dad is leaning into a crowbar. Ivy's wheelchair ramp – what's left of it – twists crookedly away from the wall. Gaping bolt holes scar the bricks where the ramp used to be attached to the house. The delphiniums and coreopsis and other plants lie crushed on the ground. Dark circles of sweat soak the armpits of Dad's t-shirt.

"What are you doing?" I yell. My heart is pounding like a jack-hammer.

"Taking down the ramp. What's it look like I'm doing?"

My bike crashes to the ground and I charge across the garden.

"It's not enough that you…you…" I shove Dad hard into the brick wall. "You drowned her, didn't you!"

Dad opens his mouth but I cut him off.

"I might have been one lousy brother but I would *never* have done what you did!" And I smash my fist hard into his face. His nose flattens under my knuckles.

I watch the blood gush. And then – for my sister, for Ivy – I smash him again.

Just then Hannah rounds the corner of the house. She's changed out of her running clothes but looking all grubby. Dad swipes an arm across his face, leaving a streak of blood. "She's been helping stack the lumber. She—"

"*Yoo-ou*—!" I bellow at her. "*You traitor!*"

"David," Hannah says, moving over beside my dad. "It's not like that. I just—"

My feet pound the pavement hard. Down the side-walk and past the end of our street. A sharp, angry smell rises off my body. How could she go help him, knowing what he did? How could she help him wreck the one thing left of Ivy's?

And my garden! How *could* she?

Chapter 26

My chest feels like someone's running a buzz saw through it. My shins are screaming. I can't run any farther. I can hardly walk. I stumble through the streets not caring if I look like a madman.

Even if I could run forever, I'll never escape how it felt to see Hannah standing beside my dad. After telling me, not more than an hour before, that she knew I'd told her the truth about him. After letting me hold her.

The only person who ever really cared about me is Ivy. And Will.

I duck into a variety store and ask to use their phone.

"I'd love to see you, David," Will says. "One of the

staff here is taking me to the botanical gardens this afternoon. How about I meet you there?"

It feels so good just to hear his voice. I should have called him ages ago.

At the entrance to the botanical gardens, I hand over some of my school-supply money.

The perennial beds here look tired. Or maybe it's just me that's tired. I've got a lot of time to kill before meeting Will, so I take a deep breath and turn along a path I haven't taken before. It's lined with lilies. Butterflies flit from one to another. The lilies smell different outside than they did in the church at Ivy's funeral.

Will everything be defined now in terms of Ivy and how she died?

Apples in the orchard are starting to turn red. I haven't been here since the trees were blooming. When life was simple but I didn't know it. Before Ivy died. Before I met Hannah.

The path through the lily beds leads to a shady area where speckled lungwort carpets the ground under spruce trees. Lungwort's Latin name, *Pulmonaria*, sounds much better. The bottom branches of the spruce trees have been removed so people can walk underneath them. This afternoon I'm the only one here.

I should have brought Ivy here. She would have liked how the sunlight dances in patches where it's filtered through the tall trees. She was always noticing stuff like that. And giggling. Like she did in the bath. Even if you didn't know what she was giggling about, when Ivy giggled, it made you want to giggle, too.

That was enough to make her life worthwhile, wasn't it? Worthwhile for her?

Or was Ivy's life tougher than I ever let myself believe? How do you weigh crappy stuff like seizures and physio and people hardly ever understanding you, up against giggles and grins and just being happy with birds and pretty flowers and your sunhat and your turquoise bathing suit? How can anyone know whether someone else's life is worth living or not, especially if that someone can't tell you about it?

The formal garden I've wandered into is mostly roses. The paths between the beds are straight lines. As soon as I see a way out, I take it, and wander instead into a wilder looking area of meadow grasses and ponds.

Would dying seem like not such a bad thing if you believed in heaven? Hannah's idea of heaven sounds better than the idea of angels singing and playing harps and stuff. The day of Ivy's funeral she said she thought heaven could be different things for different people. Like for me it might be a garden and for Dad it might be someplace where he could actually live like the ancient Greeks and Romans, and not just give lectures about them.

In the shade of a large maple, I spot a bench and sit down. I've been wandering the gardens for a long time and I was beat before I started.

On a nearby pond, water lilies open their petals to the pale sun. *Nymphaea* something – I forget what the white ones are called. Perched on their shiny leaves, fat frogs bask in the warmth. Dragonflies dart back and forth over the surface of the water.

A warm breeze strokes my face, my hands feel heavy, resting beside me on the bench. On the far side of the pond cattails sway, and I feel my eyes beginning to close.

From far across a huge field, Ivy is running toward me with a pack of dogs – little, big, red, yellow, and blue – just like the dogs in her favorite book. There's one brown dog, too. As clearly as anyone anywhere has ever spoken, Ivy calls out, "Is that you, Livingston?"

The brown dog barks, "To the tree!" And into the tree Ivy flies like a bird.

The dogs in the tree are wearing hats. Ivy shouts, "A dog party!"

Something tickles the back of my hand. A feather from a party hat.

I open my eyes.

A dragonfly has landed on my hand. Its eyes are huge. They take up a good part of its head. And I can see how each separate leg is attached to the dragonfly's long slender body. Its wings are like stained glass, a bunch of tiny panes all knit together with intricate black lines. Ivy would have noticed the tiny rainbows in the wings that are both delicate and strong. They sparkle in the sun as the dragonfly leaves my hand.

Water laps against the reeds growing at the edge of the pond. Water, lapping the shore.

Too bad my dream of Ivy's heaven was just that. A dream.

"Do you mind if we join you here?" Two nuns smile down at me.

"No, it's okay," I say, getting up. "I was just leaving. Seriously. Nothing personal." I hurry then around the pond and through the Japanese garden toward the tea house.

Just approaching the door as I get there, is a woman pushing an old man in a wheelchair. I don't recognize him at first, till he lifts a hand and smiles. "David!"

The woman with him says, "You must be the young man Mr. Paley has been telling me about. I can't tell you how pleased he was that you called today. I'll leave you two to chat alone for a while. Say, half an hour?"

"Sure. Yeah." The sight of Will in a wheelchair is still a bit of a shock.

The tea house hostess leads us to a table on the patio. When she goes to move a chair to make room for Will, he says, "I'd like to be facing the coreopsis, please."

"You always did like the yellow flowers best, eh?" I settle in across the table. "So, Will, what's with the wheelchair?"

Will shakes his head. "My first night in the home, I fell going into the bathroom."

"I guess it was good you were there then."

Will dismisses my comment with a shaky flick of his hand. "You didn't call me up today to talk about the foolish frailties of an old man. Tell me, what are your new neighbors like? Nice people living in my old house, I hope?"

I can't bring myself to talk about Hannah. Not now.

"Yeah. Turns out it's someone Mom used to know."

Will orders tea and I order a root beer. We talk a bit about the library at the seniors' home – it's so-so – and the meals. Pretty good. We talk about school starting up soon and music the choir might do this year. The waitress brings us our drinks and Will gets me to do the sugar in his tea. Tapping his fingers together, he says, "I've lost a little something here. Coordination." He asks me about my garden.

Again the image of Dad and Hannah among the broken plants and the wreckage of Ivy's ramp. "He let her go, Will. In the lake. Dad let Ivy go."

Will's eyebrows shoot up, then he looks down into his tea. "I was sorry to hear about your sister, David, and I was surprised when I didn't hear from you sooner. I was sorry not to get to her funeral, too, but I was in rough shape for a while after my fall. I would have sent a card, but..."

I wonder if he heard what I said, and think maybe it would be better if he didn't. It's not something I was planning to say, when I called him. I wasn't planning anything. I just wanted to see him. I take a long sip of my drink. Will lifts his cup in two hands and sets it down again.

When he finally looks up at me, his gaze is direct. "I wish I'd been brave enough to do something for my Vera." His wife. Before she died, her Alzheimer's was so bad she didn't know who he was anymore.

Behind Will, pincushion flowers nod their blue heads.

"I never thought of it like that. But Will—?" I swallow hard and tell him carefully, "Will, it's not the same."

He licks his dry lips, rubs his hand across his face and says, "No. You're right, David. It's not."

Neither of us seems to know what to say after that, but we've spent lots of time together not talking, just watching TV or gazing at gardens, so I think we're okay. I hope I haven't wrecked everything that was easy about us, blurting out about Dad and everything.

I see Will's caregiver coming along the path back to the tea house, carrying a bag from the gift shop. "I'm glad we met up today," I tell him.

"Me too," Will says, and before we say good-bye, he makes me promise I'll come see him at the home.

As I'm leaving the botanical gardens, dark clouds cover the sun. Before I'm half way home, it looks as if the sky could open up any minute. I duck into the library and settle into a corner with a book about trees. Who knew there's a species of tree that was destroyed in the Ice Age everywhere except in China? *Gingko biloba*. If a bunch of Buddhist monks hadn't planted them around their temples, they'd be extinct. I should come back when I have my card sometime. Take the book with me when I go see Will.

I leave the library when the rain stops. The setting sun reflects brilliantly off the wet sidewalks and streets as I trudge slowly in the direction of home. Car tires hiss along the wet pavement. The humidity is gone from the air.

Along the front of our house where Ivy's ramp used to be, muddy footprints are filled with rainwater. Dad's footprints and Hannah's. Around the empty space, shrubs have been trampled and blossoms crushed. I look for the odd-looking plant among them but I can't find it. And I can't yet go inside and face Dad. I can't.

Chapter 27

This late in the day, the playground is empty. Maybe I should have gone in for supper but I wouldn't have been able to eat anyway.

With the bottom edge of my t-shirt I dry off the seat of a swing and jump on. I pump my legs and pull hard on the chains, sending myself as far as I can from the ground and the blur of neighboring houses and dog-walkers who didn't get out earlier because of the rain. Back and forth I go, kicking hard into the leafy canopy of a nearby oak. Back and forth until the chains blister my hands.

"I went looking for you but I couldn't find you."

Beside the swings are Hannah and Shamus. I feel lightheaded, but pump harder anyway.

She calls up to me again. "I understand why you were mad."

"Oh really?"

"I was still trying to fit everything together. You know, what I thought I knew about your dad and what you told me? And when I was getting dressed after my shower, I saw him. Out there in front of your house. All in a rage, it looked like, ripping apart the ramp."

"That's great, Hannah." I yank hard on the chains. "I can see *exactly* why that would make you go over to help."

"Give me a break, David, would you?" she calls up to me. "I'm trying to explain."

Shamus is pulling on his leash toward some dogs running free at the other end of the park.

"It shocked me," Hannah says. I'm too tired, too pissed off with everyone to hear any more, but swinging back and forth with Hannah below me, what can I do? "The violence of what he was doing. It didn't fit with how I'd seen him, you know? Holding Ivy at your cottage? Cupping the back of her head so gently? Talking to her so sweetly? I wanted to try and understand, so I went over."

My blisters sting. I feel like throwing up. I wish Hannah would shut up and go away. Instead she bends down to unhook Shamus's leash. He hurtles across the park toward the other dogs.

"And now you do?" I ask her. "You get it now?"

"No."

That's something anyway.

"But I keep thinking about the seizure Ivy had by the bonfire," she says, "and I wonder, if the one she had in the water with your dad…Well, it might have been even worse. And even if it wasn't, even if it was just the same… Well…" She looks up at me.

I'm still swinging back and forth and I could barf any minute.

"I thought maybe your dad wouldn't have been able to save Ivy, even if he tried. Even if he tried really hard. I just wanted to tell you that," Hannah says, her voice trailing off. "In case it helps at all."

From across the park comes a furious barking.

"Shamus, come!"

The dog moseys back across the park, sniffing another dog or two along the way.

The contorted grimace on Ivy's face highlighted by the glow of the bonfire. The violent wracking of her limbs. Maybe Hannah's right. Maybe Dad couldn't have saved her. My arms are trembling from gripping the chains for so long.

The thing is, he didn't even try.

Hannah clips Shamus's leash back onto his collar and says, "There's one other thing I've been thinking. You probably won't agree but—"

No more.

I jump.

The jolt of landing jars me through my knees straight up to my teeth. I'm still off balance when Shamus yanks toward me, leans against me, and knocks me over onto the wet grass.

"David, I'm so sorry!" Hannah says. But she's laughing and Shamus is wagging his whole back end and licking my face like mad.

Then he plunks himself down beside me as if lying around in the park together is something we do all the time, and what can I do but laugh, too?

When Hannah kneels down beside him and strokes his coat, her hand brushes against my side. A light breeze lifts wisps of her hair as she looks off in the distance, her face in silhouette against the setting sun.

And I just lie there on the damp grass, with my arm around Hannah's dog, aware of her hand, resting now between Shamus and the beating of my heart.

Chapter 28

Hannah unfolds herself and gets up from the ground. "I was on my way to the cemetery when I saw you here," she says. "Would you want to go with me?"

"You go there?"

"I've been a couple of times."

I'd go anywhere with her just to hold onto the sense of her fingers against my shirt a while longer, even if her theory about Dad and Ivy doesn't do anything for me.

The streets are quiet as we make our way to the cemetery, and so are we. The sun is getting low in the sky by the time we get there, softly filtering sideways through the trees.

Hannah kneels beside Ivy's grave, holding Shamus's leash loosely while he sniffs at the fresh earth.

"David, can I ask you something?"

"Yeah."

"Ivy really liked the water, didn't she."

"You know she did. You were there."

"If she hadn't died in the lake, how—?"

"Hannah, I really don't want to talk about Ivy anymore." I kneel on the ground beside her. "I just can't. Okay? Can we just...not talk?"

"Sorry." She turns her face away.

"I didn't mean...It's just..."

She flexes her fingers. "No it's okay. Really." She looks back at me and sort of half smiles. I really have missed her.

I know what she was getting at. If Ivy hadn't died in the lake with Dad that day, she would probably have died in a hospital eventually. Ivy hated the hospital, so looking at it that way, dying in the water had to be better. Especially if she went quickly. Which she might have. Kind of how things went for Livingston maybe.

But even if it was like that — and maybe it wasn't — did that make it okay for Dad to do what he did? To decide — whatever made him decide — that her life would now end? Sure, she's free of all the crap life handed her.

But didn't she deserve more chances to splash in her bath and laugh at Shamus's tricks? To talk to the birds and eat orange gummy bears?

Gummy bears. Not worms.

"Hannah, I did something once. Something awful." I don't have to tell her this. She might even write me off if I do. I know I don't matter to her like Dad does. But I do have to tell her. "I got mad at Ivy once. A long time ago."

I pick up a handful of earth and crumble it between my fingers.

"I was supposed to go to a kid's birthday party, but Ivy got sick and messed things up so I couldn't go. So I went out to Mom's garden – it was still hers then – and I dug up some worms. Earthworms. Big fat ones."

Hannah is holding herself very still beside me. I don't dare look at her.

"They were wriggling and moist and I took them, and I fed them to Ivy. All of them. I put them in her mouth. One after another. Even after worm guts were sticking to her teeth and her lips."

The sun has almost disappeared and Hannah still hasn't taken off.

"That's how much I hated her that day. After I did it, I wasn't mad at her anymore. But I never said I was sorry or anything because I wasn't. Not then. Not really."

I never intended to tell Hannah all that, I was never going to tell anyone any of it, but now that I have…"I wasn't really sorry until this summer, after Ivy was gone, and I couldn't tell her anymore."

I look at Hannah then, breathing softly beside me. She just bites her bottom lip and says, finally, "You're human, David."

On the far side of the cemetery, in the fading light, a couple is pushing a stroller. A little kid marches along behind them, bashing a stick against the ground.

"It's getting dark," Hannah says. "Should we be heading home?"

When we stand up, a lone bird flies out of the canopy of leaves above our heads and into the gathering darkness. *Eep eeep*.

Walking slowly toward the cemetery gates, Hannah reaches across the space between us. She takes my hand.

And that's when I trip on a bump in the road.

She doesn't even laugh.

Her grip on my hand is strong. Her fingers intertwine with mine. The skin between them is soft. I squeeze her hand and she squeezes back.

When I get home, Mom meets me in the kitchen.

"Your dad's gone to bed early," she says. I just shrug and she urges me to eat something. I realize I haven't eaten all day so I let her make me a ham sandwich. As I put my plate in the dishwasher she says, "Are you okay, David?"

"Yeah, sure."

"We will be," she says. "We have to believe that."

I nod. "Okay."

"Goodnight then, David."

After I'm ready for bed, I go stand at the front door and turn on the outside light. The bird feeder leans crookedly in the middle of the mess out there and there's no way to get down to the garden. I turn the light off again. Stars glitter brightly in the black sky. As I turn to go to my room, the craziest thought occurs to me.

The thing Ivy had about birds all summer…Could she have seen the gulls in the sky over the lake that day and decided, herself, that it was time to join them?

A nice idea. My sister, ready to die, flying off with the birds up to heaven. Whatever heaven might be for her.

And it is crazy.

But is it any crazier than what Hannah or my mom have come up with to get them through all that's happened to us this summer?

Probably.

Chapter 29

The sun is already well up in the sky when I stir the next morning.

Standing at Ivy's window – the living room window – I see that Dad is outside. He's gathering stalks and branches that got wrecked when he took Ivy's ramp down. There's a look of grim determination on his face as he stuffs the debris into a bin.

I've had so many theories about what he did, and listened to so many attempts to make sense of it – none of them making sense – that all I feel anymore is raw. As if all my insides have been scraped with a knife and rubbed with salty gravel.

Across the street, Hannah's front door opens and out bounds Shamus. He runs to the driveway, snaps up the rolled newspaper in his mouth, then bounds across the quiet street and drops it on the ground beside Dad. If Dad even notices, it doesn't register on his face as he rams his arm down into the bin of debris.

From her front step, Hannah shouts, "Bring it home, Shamus! Come!"

The dog again grabs the paper and bounds back across the street. When he delivers it to Hannah, she takes hold of his collar, waves to me, and goes back inside.

The damage done to most of the plants isn't as bad as I had thought. The mock orange and the mugho pine will grow new branches. That odd-looking plant I don't know the name of – it's still there, just leaning a bit lopsided, like the bird feeder. The coreopsis and delphiniums will bloom again in another season.

But something has to be done, soon, about the gaping space where the ramp used to be. I could map out a garden there and plant it all myself. With a bit of help, I could probably even build steps.

Dad looks to be contemplating that area now, but he wouldn't have a clue where to start designing a garden. He takes a trowel from his back pocket and slowly begins trying to level the earth that has been gouged by heavy feet and ends of lumber.

After a few minutes, he sits back on his heels, as I've often sat myself, working alone in this garden. Dad's alone out there now. As alone as he was in the water with Ivy that day, when he let her go. And as alone as he's been ever since, even if Mom hasn't left him.

What he's doing out there is pretty feeble. But he is trying to do something. I have to give him that. He's out there alone and making the best he can of the messes he's made. For me? Maybe. Because maybe he's already done what he could for Ivy?

I don't know. I probably never will. I also don't know how any of us will ever get through all the messes we've made. But maybe I have to do what Dad's doing. Maybe I have to at least try, even if it hurts my chest just to take a deep breath and open the door.

It's a long way from the front door to the ground, but I make the leap. Dad's standing with his hands on the sides of the bin he's been filling. When my feet thud to the ground, he turns in my direction, then turns away.

It would be so easy for me to just go around to the side door and go back in the house, or head down the driveway and hide out at the botanical gardens or the library again till school gives me a better excuse to be away from here all day. But I force myself to take another deep breath and step forward into the garden.

"Hang on, Dad." I take hold of one side of the bin stuffed with debris. "You don't have to carry that yourself."

He looks at me for a long moment and says, "Thank you, David."

We haul it into the backyard and dump it. We're rounding the corner of the house, coming back out front, when a cop car pulls up at the curb.

"Mr. Burke?"

"Yes."

"Mr. Burke, a witness has come forward who says he saw you in the water with your daughter. I'm afraid we're going to have to take you in for questioning."

Chapter 30

Dad goes willingly. Mom follows in the van. I'm fine with that. Sort of. I mean, I could have gone too, if I wanted, but I don't need to be part of whatever comes next.

I finish cleaning up what Dad started, disposing of damaged plant material, and raking level the ground closest to the house. I already have ideas for how we should build steps to the door – stone, I think – and what would grow well around them.

It's funny. When Mom first made me take on the weeding a couple of years ago and got me to re-edge the beds, I hated doing it. But I don't mind any of it now. The garden is one place I actually don't mind being alone. Alone with the *bi-yee fars. Eep eep.*

I straighten up the bird feeder, refill it, then I take the clippers to the back garden, and snip an armful of sunflowers – *Helianthus*.

I carry them across the handlebars of my bike to the cemetery and lay them on my sister's grave.

"Ivy," I tell her, "it's not better here without you."

Nearby, a new gravesite is being dug. The air smells earthy and damp.

"And Ivy, I'm sorry – about stuff I did. Especially about the worms."

The morning light casts shadows over the name carved into Ivy's simple headstone. A different light from what I've seen here before.

I don't know what's going to happen next. I guess Dad will be charged. With something. And I guess there'll be a trial. But will any judge or jury be able to figure out better than I can what should happen next?

I don't know.

Acknowledgments

Thanks first and foremost to my steadfast partner-in-life, Peter Carver, who read pages and read them again, offered his feedback and encouragement, listened endlessly as I mulled aloud, counseled me on editorial, strategic, and emotional matters, and tolerated hours and years of my preoccupation with countless versions of this story. Without his unflagging confidence in me when I was in danger of losing it completely, I don't know that this project would have ever become the novel it now is.

Thanks to writer-friends who read the entire manuscript, in some cases many times, and provided invaluable feedback and encouragement – Lena Coakley, Hadley Dyer, Paula Wing, Ted Staunton, Rob Morphy, Nan Forler, and Heather Smith. Thanks also to my daughter Kelly Stinson and my grandson Michael Greenlaw who also read the manuscript and offered new and helpful ways of thinking about the characters and the situations they faced.

Thanks to another writer-friend, Joanne Jaques, who introduced me to Noel Daley when I needed him most, and to Noel Daley himself. During years when drafts of the novel took the outcome of Ivy's death many months (and in some drafts years) beyond where it has ended up, he provided countless willing hours on the phone with me, sharing his knowledge of the legal system and how it works. I hope someday to write a book that will begin to make use of all the insights he so generously shared.

Thanks also to Janet Barclay, Bill Millar, Richard Ungar, Jim Kitchens, and Mike Thomas.

And thanks to the great team at Second Story Press – Margie Wolfe, Carolyn Jackson, Melissa Kaita, and Emma Rodgers – for their belief in me and this book and for their help in making it what it is. Thanks also to my editor, Jonathan Schmidt.

Finally, but of no small significance, thanks to the Ontario Arts Council which provided financial support at crucial stages during the writing of this book.

About the Author

Kathy Stinson grew up in Toronto, sorted mail, taught school and waited tables before figuring out, while at home with her two children, that what she really wanted to do was write. In the years since, she has published more than 30 titles – picture books, young adult novels, historical fiction, short stories, biography, and other non-fiction. Many of her books have won awards, including *101 Ways to Dance*, which was a CLA YA Book of the Year nominee. Mother, stepmother, and grandmother, CNIB and CODE volunteer and member of CANSCAIP and TWUC, Kathy currently lives in Rockwood, Ontario with her partner, Peter Carver and their doodle, Keisha.